ALL US SAINTS

BY THE SAME AUTHOR

Still Life

ALL US SAINTS

A Novel

KATHERINE PACKERT BURKE

BLOOMSBURY PUBLISHING
NEW YORK • LONDON • OXFORD • NEW DELHI • SYDNEY

BLOOMSBURY PUBLISHING
Bloomsbury Publishing Inc.
1359 Broadway, New York, NY 10018, USA
50 Bedford Square, London, WC1B 3DP, UK
Bloomsbury Publishing Ireland Limited,
29 Earlsfort Terrace, Dublin 2, D02 AY28, Ireland

First published in the United States 2026

ISBN: HB: 978-1-63973-811-3; EBOOK: 978-1-63973-812-0

Library of Congress Cataloging-in-Publication Data is available

2 4 6 8 10 9 7 5 3 1

Typeset by Westchester Publishing Services
Printed in the United States by Lakeside Book Company

For Mom, Dad, and Chris

To plant a family! This idea is at the bottom of most of the wrong and mischief which men do.

—NATHANIEL HAWTHORNE, *THE HOUSE OF THE SEVEN GABLES*

This helps explain why television programs about violent death can feel so strangely soothing: they teach us that even the most senseless crimes can be interpreted and, ultimately, explained. That fantasy of omniscience is not all that different from the appeal of a dollhouse.

—RACHEL MONROE, *SAVAGE APPETITES*

The idea is that, to keep one world intact, you must shut all others out.

—K. PATRICK, *MRS. S*

DRAMATIS PERSONAE

EDNA ST. CLOUD, 36. Eldest daughter; twin; massacre survivor; photographer.

ROGER MERRILOW, 46. Edna's husband; successful true-crime writer.

WREN BEATRICE MERRILOW, 15. Edna and Roger's daughter; homeschooled.

CALLA ST. CLOUD, 27. New Yorker; playwright.

JAMES ST. CLOUD, 25. Youngest; video store clerk; lives up north, but visits home regularly.

HEATHER, 26. James's girlfriend of four years; baker.

SARAH FLETCHER, 20. A local.

THE MONSTER.

SETTING

May 31 of 2011 and 2012. The sprawling St. Cloud family home at 507 Hackberry Road, nestled on the edge of a park in a small Virginia city.

PROLOGUE

HOUSE LIGHTS UP

NONE OF THE St. Clouds call it a mansion. Proximity normalizes its enormity. The land around it, the woods and park, as familiar as the backyard. It is the place they grew up. It is home—this brick house at 507 Hackberry Road, vaster than even our cast can make use of.

Outsiders hold their breath as they hurry past. Any of the dozen windows could hold a ghost; every dim form is a knife-wielding scion of evil, eager to steal their bodies. The younger St. Clouds grew up hearing children chant their brother's name in playground murder ballads. The name Roland St. Cloud synonymous with deviance, and makeshift occultism, and threats to fair flesh. Thirty minutes, three bodies, a night in May near the end of the twentieth century.

There is no such thing as a haunted house, but certain places are *wrong*.

SEE FROM THE street how the lights come on. It is like one, then four, then a dozen eyes opening. See the roaming shadows—more of them than usual on this, the killings' anniversary.

Those who left must return: see James St. Cloud and his girlfriend, Heather, driving down the interstate's warming corridor. James chatters about a movie called *The House of the Devil*, its pitch-perfect pastiche of eighties horror; the small irony of this title, as he heads home, is lost on him. Heather fusses with her thumbs and only just speaks. She has never come to the house on Hackberry Road. James is reticent about what this anniversary entails—though she, like everyone, knows the story. She saw the movie, *Dollmaker*, when she was still in high school. Knew James, before they ever met, through the tiny child actor who played him. But there are more complicated things they are not talking about. If only there were something besides the rumble of the road, the muted sounds of college radio. If only they were not getting steadily closer.

See Calla St. Cloud, trying every five minutes to connect to Amtrak Wi-Fi. James had offered to drive her from New York (*It's literally on the way*, he said, *I mean, why not?*), but she couldn't stand the thought of seven hours in a car with any couple. All the *Remember when?* and inside jokes, the lovey-dovey bullshit of people who believe in permanence. Calla regrets agreeing to come home; she has skipped the anniversary's reunion these seven years since their parents died. But New York has become oppressive since she stopped writing. She stopped paying attention to the play she had running off-Broadway, stopped looking for men to fuck. She has been indoors playing *The Neighborhood*—the same game she's failing to run on Amtrak's shitty internet—and she can do that anywhere. At least at Edna's, someone else might cook for her. The game crashes again; she spits, hisses. No one sits beside her.

See the house lights: the kitchen's fluorescent glare, the living room's soft yellow. The pantry has its own bulb and window. Edna St. Cloud goes from room to room turning all of them on. Not for safety and not because it's dark. The evening's ritual hasn't begun. It is the comfort of cause and effect. The flick of a switch, the reliable binary. She can't believe her luck: tonight the whole family will be together again. Legally the house is hers—willed to her and her alone when their parents died—but spiritually it belongs to every St. Cloud. Everyone except—except—she won't think his name.

More lights: the red in her darkroom, the attic's bare bulb. There's only one room that can't be lit, bricked up these nineteen years and plastered over. Though he is not dead, Roland has no home to come back to. From outside, you'd have to know what you were looking for to spot his old bedroom.

See Roger Merrilow hemmed in by the packed shelves of his study, skimming the book that made them all famous. How strange to have lived in this house for seven years! These halls and rooms bounded by basement and attic, which he once described to the ravenous public—now more familiar to him than any former home. It is the murders' nineteenth anniversary but only their seventeenth ritual. Only after the dust settled, and the book was published, did they begin. Still—seventeen chances to perfect his monologue's cadence. He is sure of his abilities as a raconteur. But he has been distracted; it is good to brush up on his narrative. To return.

The world turns. Blue twilight falls on the yard, the brick path, the tarp-covered circle of stones in the backyard. A window is obscured. The steady sound of hammering reigns over the house, dully clear in the yard, as plywood is secured over the living room's fragile glass. This room, Edna protects above all others. This room where no one died.

Sound carries inconsistently in the St. Cloud house. Sometimes you can hear every footfall, every latching door. Sometimes every word stays in the room where it's spoken. Wren Merrilow, the youngest, takes no notice of the hammering. She has lain in bed all day, reading. She has never known a life without the ritual. It will be nice to have a full house. Since Roger started homeschooling her, she's had little contact with anyone but her parents. She has not seen her aunt, the playwright, since she was a child. And she delights in her uncle's tales from the video store—gory masterpieces she will never watch. They are a family of storytellers, Wren thinks. Even her mother's photographs are weighted with history and narrative.

It's almost night, and all the lights are on. Each door's key fills its lock. Soon the St. Clouds will move through the house, checking every dusty cranny, and—only when they know each room to be safe—finally flicking the lights off. Then the ritual can begin.

If not for the yearly ritual, Edna thinks, what would bind them together? What would bring them home? The family would drift apart, a plate tectonics of the bloodline. Calla wouldn't be on her way now. James would visit unreliably. Wren would get further away, and Roger probably. Edna would be alone in the forty-watt light with her memories of blood.

James and Heather are greeted at the door with cries of joy, *How are you*s, hugs and handshakes. What's the latest: *What are you watching, what are you reading? How's the bakery, how's school, it's a shame about the gallery*. This is what it means to come back. A return to familial flow—to all the things you share. Where you can find your way in the dark to a glass of water. It is all a ritual, every time, no matter the date.

Everyone is in the kitchen when Calla's cab pulls up. She doesn't knock; it's been seven years and she still has her key. But she knows better than to enter anonymously. Her voice echoes through the house, through the guest rooms and bathrooms, the red darkroom and study, through all the lit corners. "It's me," she says. "I'm home."

ACT I

NINETEEN YEARS AFTER

ONE

EDNA, ALONE IN the middle of the living room. She holds a walkie-talkie near her mouth even when silent. Asks: "Where is everyone now?"

The voices come back muffled with static.

James: "Upstairs bathroom's clear."

Roger: "Church-quiet in the master bedroom."

"Wren?"

"Nothing in Dad's study. I even looked under the couch."

"Locked the door behind you?"

"Yes, Mom."

"Good girl."

Lights flick off throughout the house, boxes ticked. Edna paces. Like all necessary rituals, this has not become simpler. There is always the fear until it ends. There is always the fear after.

But the living room is safe. The plywood over the windows, the shelf of books birthed by the murders: Roger's, and his shallow copycats. There is the movie and its sequels and *their* imitators—gifts from James that she hasn't seen. A violent death inspires repetition. The murders beget stories that turn back and alter the murders.

James's voice again: "Piano room's good to go."

And Roger: "Nothing in the attic but the dust and the mice." He coughs, waits, holds the line so that no one else can speak. "Eddie, we really ought to get rid of some of this."

"Later, Roger." A bit lip, a moment before the bookshelves. "Um, Heather?"

Heather's voice, practically a stranger's. "Guest room's good!"

"Great. Thank you."

James: "I'll meet you on the landing, H."

It's hard having a new person here. The last person added to the ritual was Wren, for God's sake, and she's fifteen now. But Edna is happy that James and Heather have each other. James is the one with a shot at normal life.

"Roger?"

"Nothing hides in the cupboard under the stairs but spiders."

The most threatening room is the one nobody can check. That bedroom—bricked up, sealed so tight they cannot so much as breathe its air. Her brother's things were donated or, more likely, destroyed, but Edna pictures it all still there: the desk, the dolls, the rumpled bed. Gathering dust. Waiting to erupt from the dark.

"Wren?" Edna says.

"I checked the laundry chute."

"Okay, everyone, I think—"

"Did—" Heather's voice cuts out.

"What?"

"—n—unlock the window?"

"The *what*?"

"The window in the guest room. I'll close—"

Edna's heart is rabbit, rat, and sparrow—some tiny snared thing that can only flutter at its ties or gnaw its leg off. "Everyone back, back, back." She is pulled in every direction at once but never out of the living room. She grabs a poker from the fireplace. She tugs at the plywood one-handed. To see more clearly, to escape, or some unreasoning reason. "Everyone back to the living room *now*. Wrennie, come—"

"I unlocked it." A beat. James's voice lingers three or four breaths. "The window." No one needed clarification. "It was me." Her fingers worry the plywood like a scab. "Sorry, Ed."

Deep breaths. Five things she can see: the bookshelves, Roger's record collection, assorted paperweights, the photo of Wren on the mantel, these floorboards never touched by blood. Four things she can feel: the poker's weight, the cool wall against her neck. A splinter in the arch of her foot. The scar's white furrow an inch below her clavicle; in cold weather, it sometimes aches, and her arm stiffens, but now it is painless—only skin. She hears the footsteps pause in the darkening house around her. The frogs out back singing through the trees. It has been nineteen years. Nineteen years.

"Roger," Edna says, "reset the security system when we wrap up."

Heather apologizes haltingly: she didn't mean—but Wren interrupts.

"Aunt Calla? How's your room looking?"

"It isn't *my* room." Calla's voice is bell-clear. Theatrical in its elocution. You hear four words and understand that most people would give her anything she wants. That honeystraw lilt made boys fall in love with her in high school, made girls want to be her friend or be her. They gave her love letters and paintings, gave her the clothes from their closets. When did she become so bitter, Edna would like to know. Why keep away from home for so long?

"Well," says Wren, "I can't very well ask, 'How's the room that isn't yours?' Because that would include all kinds of rooms you have no idea about."

Roger clears his throat into his walkie. "I think what dear Wren means is, ahh, no sign of anything nefarious? No—ah, intruders?"

Calla clears her throat in imitation. "Predators, would you say?"

"Well, sure."

"None in here, Rodge."

Edna holds her breath. She's lost count of whatever she can hear, see, smell. Remnants of a fire in the chimney. The reheated Indian takeout picked up yesterday in preparation. Every door is locked or will be soon. It's been nineteen years. She breathes out.

The family is all together behind the brick walls. They have never been safer. Edna says, "Okay, guys. Everyone come back so we can begin. Grab the candles, Roger." Does anyone live a life without terror? "And don't forget to check the alarm."

TWO

ALL IN THE living room. Wren, Calla, Heather, and James hold lit candles. In the dimmed light, six half-shadows flicker in a line.

Heather takes in the living room's collection of extravagant, useless things: a set of ivory chessmen stashed under the card table, a bowl of seed pearls left like an offering before a leatherbound set of Bernard Shaw. A shelf of perfect-bound plays, written by the St. Cloud parents. A framed tintype, austere St. Clouds of auld, hangs on the wall. It is a relief to have been brought here. To see, after years of imagining, the place that James grew from. There has to be some solution in these things, some cleaner understanding, if she can only piece it together.

Roger does not need to clear his throat or call for attention in order to begin. He is a man accustomed to being heard. "May 31, 1992," he says. "The night begins here. Parents in Charlottesville for the night—a workshop production of their show *Odd Man Out*. Little Calla St. Cloud, age eight, and littler James, age six, go with them. The twins, Edna and Roland, are old enough to leave behind."

Roger is the only person allowed to say the boy's name tonight. For everyone else, it's like the medieval bear taboo: say his name and he will appear.

"Edna invites over three friends: Vera Brankowski, Polly Sinclair, and Bea Fulton. Friendless Roland is in his room alone and no one thinks much of this. The girls order pizza. They fake-flirt with the delivery boy and make crank calls to their crushes. They play truth or dare while the midnight monster movie blinks across the large TV. At some late hour, Vera proposes a séance.

"'My Russian grandmother taught me how,' she says, and tutors the others in its requirements. They claim sage from the spice rack. A granite mortar, a book of matches. Everyone must contribute something to burn. It's by this burning that they will reach the world of spirits."

Calla was a teenager the last time she heard this spiel. In those days, their parents each held a candle—as grimly attended as a human sacrifice. She'd always assumed it was from their parents they learned not to sleep on this night. Even if they tried to catch it, sleep evaded them. But the shadows were there beneath Mom and Dad's eyes before the ritual began. Hollow stares through Roger's litany. Limitlessly watchful now that it was too late to save their daughter's friends from fame. Save their daughter from something worse. Sometimes Calla thought Edna had concocted the ritual to punish them. But they're seven years dead, and the punishment goes on.

Roger continues. "Polly offers a photo of her ex-boyfriend. Vera mashes a pearl drop earring. Edna is weighed down by choice. It is her house, after all; she could pick anything she owns. There's her childhood hair ribbon, the copy of *The Wind in the Willows* she'd read to pieces. The postcards Bea had sent from family trips to Paris and Greece and Rome—ancient buildings and ballpoint pen. The girls egg one another on—put in some blood, they say, put in your copy of *Pretty on the Inside*. Put in your eye, your soul, your childhood. Edna goes to her parents' study, finds the silver box engraved with the masks of tragedy and comedy, and selects two baby teeth from its velvet hold."

Roger thinks he would have made a good actor. He once suggested to Edna they make the ritual a proper piece of theater. They could assign roles, spread people throughout the house. *I could still act as narrator,* he said, *but we could really embody it. A true-blue séance of—*

Edna said no. It was the story. The candles. The flames. It was the remaking, making present. The control.

"Into the mortar go the teeth. Bea, not to be outdone, sneaks upstairs to Roland's room to select her sacrifice. Edna thinks she will return dragging Roland by a lead. Whatever Bea had planned, she finds the boy's room empty. She must have walked from one end to the other, studying the dolls he'd carved. Perhaps she looked them in the eyes and asked which one wanted to go. Perhaps she picked by simple lottery: Eenie meenie miney mo. Catch a tiger—

"Roland is already in his sister's closet. He is squeezing his shoulders into her old prom dress. He is already painting himself with her makeup. Testing the tip of the knife against his finger and spreading the blood over his rouged lips.

"It's only a joke, Bea decides. There are a hundred other dolls—a thousand—that Roland has made in his basement workshop. He is unlikely to notice. The doll she brings downstairs is smooth walnut with brilliant, Virgin Mary–blue eyes. Arms jointed with wire, varnish cured in the sun. The immaculate wooden body carries the distant star's warmth the way the girls' own tanned bodies will, come summer.

"'It looks like you, Bea,' Polly says.

"'Ew. Gross.' Bea drops it in the mortar like some fetid thing.

"The fire is fed on doll, teeth, pearl, and photo. There is a crematory reek. Vera leads them in closed-eye spiritual communion. 'Oh spirits, we seek your solace . . .' A fierce wind moans through the chimney. No one notices Roland sneak into the downstairs bathroom. He does not shake behind the shower curtain. One fist around the hilt of his kitchen knife, the other full of pink organza—he waits."

Roland used to carry James around on his shoulders. They chased geese in the park during the fall migration, fed them baguettes by way of apology. There were no photos of Roland from that night, only the film's killer. The patchy shaving, the Shirley Bassey song. A clownish drag of lipstick. Tan foundation with a pale face beneath it. And the knife, glinting in the dark. This is who James sees when he thinks of the geese.

The six figures, the four candles, drift into the cramped downstairs bathroom. The flames make comet tails through the air. "What later shocks Edna is how quickly it all happens. Polly goes to the bathroom and does not come back. Roland St. Cloud's knife pierces her cheek, her throat, and at last her heart." On James's prompting, Heather steps forward. Roger touches two fingers to her cheek, throat, chest. James blows out her candle. "The boy does not regard the blood on his stolen dress. He places Polly in the bathtub, cuts off her clothes, and, with an artist's hand, carves an X into each breast and her pubis."

Calla hasn't seen *Dollmaker* in years, but she remembers the premiere. The red carpet, the designer dress that Edna bought for her. Little Calla, only twelve; she had no claim to the night yet people still wanted her autograph, photos, clips of her copper hair. Her skin, her name, her blood—the mythology of her cursed genes. The pleasure was spoiled only when the movie began and the girl playing her exited the screen. Calla couldn't stop waiting for her to come back. She kept expecting, she later understood, to see herself die.

"Bea suggests the other girls hide, give Polly an old-fashioned scare. Vera shakes her head; though she lied about the Russian grandmother—her family is Polish—she takes matters of spirit too seriously for this. She steps outside for a cigarette, her only vice. The tobacco smoke like a séance of its own. Bea gives Edna a small smile. It is a quiet night. They are young and they are beautiful and their lives are going to be entwined forever. 'I'll take the basement, then,' Bea says. Polly is afraid of the dark. Edna is unsure how this hide-and-seeking is going to do anything but fracture the lovely night, but she returns to her parents' study and hides."

To this day, the old study is packed with wreckage from the St. Cloud parents' early years of love. Their mother had a fascination with windup toys, which their father bought her from the backs of magazines. There was a scrapbook of every recipe cooked in their first year of marriage. A list of every book they read aloud to each other: *Tristram Shandy* and *The Theater and Its Double* and *Lunch Poems*. Edna had wondered if it was possible to love another person too much. Nineteen years ago, she dreamed of leaving the house. She'd take her unburned talismans: *The Wind in the Willows*, the tartan scarf Bea gave her for Christmas, the medium-format Leica she'd saved up for. She'd explode into a new life with her old postcards tacked to a corkboard. She'd be kept safe by the ballpoint swooping *L*, the butterfly *B*: *Love, Bea*. Love her friends, love forever. She'd have a new life at Bard or Sarah Lawrence, or go west to Reed or Pomona, or she'd go someplace she'd never heard of. All the people she'd meet, all the life she'd make.

Well, she hadn't been wrong. She's had a life like she never dreamed.

Three candles now. Everyone in the vestibule. "Vera's is the first death Edna hears. A stifled shout, an *urk* in the entryway, the gentle thud of body and floor. It only takes a dash across the throat to kill Vera Brankowski." James offers his throat to Roger's fingers, and blows out his candle. "Roland takes his time. Vera's clothes are not cut away but unbuttoned, slipped off, piled beside her body. An X in her forehead and hands. The girl's blood stains his palms like ash."

For almost two decades, the question has echoed through Edna: How could she not have known? She was supposed to know her twin better than anyone. He had always been unsettling; Bea made jokes about him watching them through the bedroom keyhole and jerking off. But how could she know that he would cut and kill? That he would convince himself that by this killing, their bodies might be his—that he might become a girl? The closeness of twins is only a fiction. She should have smothered him in his sleep. She should have died with the people she loved.

"Edna calls to her dying friend. She comes out of the study and sees a monster standing there. A creature born in the mouth of Hell." Edna bought the dress in tenth grade when George Deakins asked her to prom. Afterward, not immune to cliché, they drove to the parkway and fucked in the back of George's car. Roland wore it badly, his hair in messy pigtails. As the knife slid into the place above her right breast, Edna thought of how gentle George had been. He should have torn the dress off her, so that it could not come back to hurt her now. "It is only after he stabs her that she sees her brother."

A hesitation, and Roger prods two fingers into Wren's shoulder. She does not waver. She knows her mother's scar like an old lullaby.

"Before the wretch can strip his sister, before he can withdraw his knife, he is interrupted by Bea Fulton. She stands, a vision in black, framed by the door and the basement's dark."

Hey, fag-boy, Bea had called out.

"She holds a rusted hammer in one hand and a doll in the other. A nun, or perhaps a saint."

Hey, pervert, the actress playing Bea says in the film. *Aren't you too old to play with dollies?*

"She tosses the doll down and beats it to pieces."

Hey, Eddie, the resurrected Bea says in one of the many sequels. *You look like you've seen a ghost.* And her rigid limbs break as wires marionette her into the mockery of a hug.

"Roland snarls. There's nothing human in the sound. Bea has another doll in hand: a minotaur with a tranquil face. 'Stop me, why don't you?' Bea yells, and runs back into the basement. The murderous creature follows."

The girl playing Bea in the film was gorgeous: blue eyes and ink-spill hair. She and Edna got drinks so the actress could ask questions about her dead friend. What Edna couldn't say was, *Look at you, in your red leather jacket. You're already perfect. You know her—she's you.* The woman won an award for her performance; Edna sent flowers but never heard from her again.

"Up above are all the world's dead and Edna, knife still stuck in her. To remove it is to risk bleeding out. To leave it in risks a far worse death. Below is upheaval. The ballpark crack of breaking wood. Tools clatter to the ground. The police will find Bea with a three-inch whittling knife stuck in her eye." Calla sneers when Roger presses his fingers to her eyelid. Knowing better than to wait for her, James blows out her candle. "Edna leaves a slug-trail of blood on the wall as she stands. When she draws out the knife, she cries loud enough to nearly wake her murdered friends. By the time Roland reaches the top of the stairs, she is ready for him. The knife goes into his chest just above his corrupted, black heart. There is a minotaur-look on his face as he grapples for the rail. Edna yanks the knife free of bone and plunges it in again. And again."

They used to have a doll representing him. They'd each stick a pin in—a burst of silver points from the cloth body. But the doll had been too grim a reminder. It was better with only words and fire. At once closer to and further from the soul of the thing.

Here at the denouement, Roger's voice is like autumn leaves—crisp, dry, and only waiting for the wind to free each word. "Finally, he fell down the long steps. There were no ghosts, no demons or ghouls. There was no evil in the world but the world itself. There was only Edna, seventeen and shaking cold, and the stairs and the blood. There was only Roland, her twin, and the wet rattle of breath drawn through his chest like a thread. An immeasurable distance between them. She thought, wrongly, he would die soon."

Wren's candle is the only light left burning. She can still feel the print of her father's fingers on her shoulder. The genetic memory of that blade. Edna doesn't bite her thumb or look to the windows. Her eyes are fixed on her brave daughter's candle flame. Still alive, still alive. Wren is the symbol, the ritual survivor, that keeps the walls standing.

Six hands on the candle, the perfect smooth wax. The heat at the top, where Edna places her hand, is nearly unbearable. They go to the kitchen, this twelve-legged creature. The artificial dead, and the true survivor, and their narrator. There is a candlestick on the kitchen table. As one, they place the lit candle inside. It will burn until sunrise. The doors are locked, the sun has set. All that's left is to wait out the darkness.

THREE

JAMES'S CHILDHOOD BEDROOM has not changed. He returns here once, twice a year, keeps the space his own. There are childhood posters for *The Texas Chain Saw Massacre* and Fall Out Boy. Photos of him as the Artful Dodger, as Jack chopping down the beanstalk. There, low on the wall: five grubby stains the span of a child's fingers. There on the desk is a small TV, a DVD player—spoils of his fifteenth birthday. He'd sat up all night watching movies with the sound off. He'd put on subtitles, or let just the wordless images—the bright, flickering faces—flash over him.

"All right, let's hear it," he says. "Let me have it straight."

"It's fun to see your childhood bedroom." Heather nods at the posters. "God, you were such an emo kid."

"You're racing for the hills. You're absolutely terrified." James folds his clothes as he sheds them, places them neatly on the desk. Heather sits on the bed, already in mint-green pajamas. She pats the space beside her. A face so sweet and sincere that James cannot look.

"It was intense," she says.

"You're going to tell Manny and Gretchen and all the rest that their old pal James comes from a family like something out of Dickens. A stale cake on the kitchen table. A wedding dress spread-eagled on the lawn going brown in the rain."

"Are *you* okay?"

"Don't change the subject." He struggles into a fresh T-shirt. "'Poor, poor, Jamie,' you'll say. You'll be standing on that stump in Gretchen's backyard, drowning your sorrows in PBR. 'We had a good thing going. We always knew his family was fucked-up, but we didn't expect them to be so *obsessed*—'"

"Hang on, James, I mean it—"

"'There was always something wrong with him. All those violent movies he rented. He'd put on Red House Painters at parties for God's sake. I guess we'll never know what becomes of him. I guess some day he'll probably shoot up a sch—'"

"James. Stop." He pauses halfway into his T-shirt, face covered. "Sit. How long has your sister been doing that?"

"Being an"—Heather tugs the shirt down for him—"obsessive freak? Forever. You get used to it."

"That's not exactly comforting."

"I said you didn't have to come."

"Look, Jamie, this isn't about me." There are words she's rehearsed—the distance she feels, the silence. The way he shrugs her off when she spoons him. And three nights ago: the sex, the skirt, the crying. It hovers over them the way stink hangs around an abattoir. Maybe they could skip to the end, the part where the crying was done. It's nothing, and they can go on with their lives; it's something, and decisions have to be made. "I love you," she says. "If this is a thing you have to do, I'm doing it with you."

Nothing from James. One of these days she's going to save him from the May 31 ritual. They'll stay home, make pizza from scratch, queue up a *Tetsuo* movie. Have Gretchen and her inevitable new girlfriend over. The night would pass—a night like any other.

She says, "Yes or no: Are you okay?"

"Right as rain."

Heather rises to check the door. Still locked. Two hollow knocks as she unlocks it, locks it again.

"What do we do now?" she asks. "Sleep?"

"You can if you want to. None of us ever do."

"You sit up all night, stewing."

"We stew in this every day, H. It runs fucking hot and cold through our veins."

You have choices to make, Heather wants to say. *You can leave it behind.*

Sitting again beside James. "Tell me about him. Your brother."

"You haven't heard enough tonight about that murdering tra—"

"Something *good*."

James thinks. Not about what, but whether to tell.

The drawers of his desk are packed with childhood's bowerbird pleasures. Doodles and shells and whippit containers he found on the elementary school playground. A duck call he never got the knack for sounding. Track lists for missing mix CDs. Between these: a flat wooden box the size of his palm. There is no obvious seam. Into one face is carved a snake biting its tail.

"Can you open this?" he asks.

Heather tries. She has seen puzzle boxes like these before, knows that there are pressure points, hidden catches. The box doesn't yield. She offers it back.

"I couldn't either," James says, not taking it. Heather keeps trying. "After the murders, once I was a little older, I thought for sure that he'd left some kind of note for me in there. He showed me how to open it, but I couldn't remember, couldn't ask him. I spent whole nights awake trying to pry it apart, shaking it by my ear and telling myself there was something rattling inside.

Something that would prove—not that he was innocent. But that it made sense. That he had always been that—monster."

"It looks impossible," Heather says. "I can only find the seam if I run my thumbnail over it."

"My brother was good at making things like that. Not just dolls. Fuck it, he was a genius. Two hours, maybe two and a half, between when he started cutting the wood and when he had it all together. He'd sneak little toys or notes to us in those puzzle boxes. He told us that every ordeal ought to have a gift at the end."

"You must have opened it once."

"Only once." He takes the box from her as if to prove he's lost the ability. "It felt like a miracle."

"Let me guess—there was nothing inside."

"No, there was." He presses and tugs and shakes the box. This would be the perfect moment, James thinks, for it to open again. For whatever divine hand once intervened to return. "It was a photo. A crumpled little Polaroid of me on Halloween. Standing next to an uncarved pumpkin as big as I was." He tosses the box back to her. "I was so mad I put it back and sealed it away."

"I wish I could see," Heather says. Thinking of that anger. Thinking about unbreakable bonds. "What about now?"

"What *about* now?"

"Do you ever bring—" Again her fingers slide over the box's polished body: it turns and turns, trapped like living prey. "I mean, I know you've visited—"

"Sure, I've brought it to him. I've chucked it in his fucking face, yelled until my voice went. It's all for nothing. There's no one there, H. He couldn't recognize this. He can't even speak."

FOUR

THE ROOM CALLA stays in was the St. Clouds' playroom. Its paint is recent but spotty. The edge of a once-smiling sun still clear in the corner. A wisteria vine sketched along the baseboard. Apart from these strays, the walls are bare and cloud-white. Gone is the trunk of costumes she and James hiked around their waists, the cardboard skies and castles. James had been good at taking directions; he didn't have the childish need to improvise his lines or alter his role. He was the evil witch abducting Calla, beheaded by play's end. He was the dog helping her girl detective catch the mailman killer. The sapling that she, lovelorn, languished beneath while her lover was at war. How happy these performances made their parents.

Now there is only the desk, the twin bed, the worn leather armchair. She sits at the desk, playing *The Neighborhood*. Her cartoon avatar—an inhuman body stretched and pointed and gray—walks around a digital re-creation of the St. Cloud home. She has seen in-game homes as lovingly decorated as any in real life: plants that spill from window boxes, ornately rendered Moroccan rugs. She has seen a complete digital set of Portmeirion dishes, a different pixeled botanical on each. Everyone in *The Neighborhood* gets a house. What's costly is furnishing it—making it a place other people might visit. But Calla's house in *The Neighborhood* is empty. Digital wind whistles through it. The steps of her spindly avatar echo down the hallways of her childhood. This is not a place to live.

She selects a match from her inventory. The player-character who sold the matches to her wanted to talk about places to camp in-game. *There's a really cool spot near the edge of the map*, they said, *where you can see all the stars*. Calla's avatar strikes the match and sets the digital house aflame.

"Knock, knock!" Roger's voice; his knuckles rap the open door.

"Isn't knocking alone indignity enough?"

Flame sprites spread through the house—across the entryway, through the guest room, the hallway, and Calla's childhood room. Down the hall, into the living room, the dining room, the kitchen. The speakers crackle like cellophane.

"How're you settling in?" Roger says.

"I mean, it's not like the door was closed. What's the point of knocking?"

"I know it may not be the, ah, most luxurious accommodations. But Wren is in your old room and—"

"And we're not all so comfortable as *you* are sharing a bed with a child." Calla quits the game, shuts her laptop.

Roger doesn't blink. "Were you writing?" he asks.

"No."

"Edna and I were sorry to miss your new play—*Shield*, was it? I heard the set design was exceptional. It's so much for Edna, you know, going back and forth to New York." Calla waits. "Your sister is very glad to have you home."

"Which is why she's the one telling me."

Roger has barely progressed beyond the doorframe. Good, thinks Calla. Let him stay uncomfortable. Let me make a space that repels him as oil does water.

"It's a difficult time for her."

"Her whole life is a difficult time," Calla says, "the way she tells it."

"Well, I hardly think that's fair. Look at what she's accomplished: A solo exhibition at the Whitney when she was twenty-five. A career retrospective at the Getty when she was thirty."

"And dropped by her gallery when she was thirty-six."

"Ah. You heard about that."

"I pay attention." Calla enjoys the way his body slackens and his face becomes drawn. A puppet with an arthritic hand up his ass. Maybe she *should* come home more often.

"Her last round of photos was, ah, very abstract," Roger says. "It's difficult work, you know. It's—"

"Dreadful."

"You saw it?"

"Like I said, I pay attention." Calla thinks she's the only one in this family with any idea how art worlds function. All those high-priced pieces laundering money for the rich, alchemically diminishing their tax burdens to zero. You don't have to be good to command high prices; you only have to have a name worth something. If Edna's gallery dropped her, it's because she's been out of fashion for years.

Roger hastens to say: "It isn't for everyone. A bit more Man Ray than Sally Mann but there's no accounting for—"

"Oh my god, you hate it too."

Roger's shock looks genuine. "Certainly not!"

"You can't lie to me, Roger. I've known you since I was nine years old."

"And how did Edna convince you to come home this year, eh?" He thinks he's so clever. "I'm sure it's a coincidence that *Shield* closed early."

Calla would have shut it down herself if she could have. She'd stopped paying attention to the performances, stopped answering the director's calls. Let it limp dead and broken past the finish line. Let it die like a child of thirst in the woods. She hadn't been able to stand the thought of those stupid, empty scenes done night after night.

She gives the biggest smile she can. "I came to see the old girl's life falling apart. I assumed there'd be fireworks."

"And what form do you imagine these fireworks might take?"

The smile stretches. "Something's going to explode."

"How's that?"

"Only joking, Rodge. Lighten up." Calla opens her computer and resumes the game. Her avatar stands in a field of ash. When a real house burns, there must be something left behind—pipes, a foundation, the bathtub that once held a dying girl. But in the game, none of that remains. Trees surround the lot on three sides; black birds flit between their branches. There is a humanoid fox pushing a stroller down the street. There is an entire world beyond, but this patch of it is Calla's and Calla's alone.

Roger moves to leave. He doesn't know why he bothers being so nice; nineteen years and Calla's always the same. But he lingers, waits to see what else she'll say. It's worth giving attention to the people who hate you. They teach you how to unmake them.

"You do have to imagine this place is haunted." Calla speaks softly enough that she could be talking to herself. "It killed Edna's friends. It killed our parents. It's like one of those dreadful movies James is always watching. *The Amityville Hogwash*." She does not look at Roger, and it's by this that he knows she is serious. "'Ghosts' being just another name for the compulsion. For something evil in the house itself. Voices whisper from the walls, dreams smother sleeping heads. Who do you think will go next, Roger? Could be you."

Calla clicks about the game, rebuilding the house from a saved set of blueprints. She's begun to think of this doubled house—this empty, burning analogue—as the Spitehouse: out of spite she burns it down; out of spite, she rebuilds. It comes back easily: the walls expand, the floors tiling like a flower unfurling. The fox person pauses their stroll to watch. The birdsong quiets. All the world watching this common miracle.

She goes on: "Did you know our mother had been hoarding sleeping pills? She must have been planning for months." Six months to second-guess. To warn her children, if she'd wanted to.

Calla was a junior in college when they found the tumor in her father's brain. Chemoresistant and too big to operate on. Calla came home only once before her mother sent him into the soft arms of death, and followed close behind. The coroner said she died an hour after he had. Was it so unbearable, that hour? Was it really so impossible to imagine living? "Can you picture her getting up in the fiery hours of the morning," Calla says, "the sun trespassing over the mountains? It wouldn't be like her to decide until the very moment. She must have looked at our father there, resting his head on the pillow beside her, and decided: today."

"Calla . . ."

"*Today I'm going to free him.* No more days of hostility and confusion. No more barfing his brains out from chemo." On that one visit, her father hadn't been doing so badly. A little cowed, a little worse at Scrabble. Why couldn't they stick it out? Why couldn't they say goodbye?

Roger says, "If you'd seen how distraught he'd been—"

"They started dying the moment one of their kids put another in the hospital. It was probably shame that made his body attack itself. The shame over what their son did, or when their daughter married that fucking pedo—"

"Enough!" Roger is angry as one is with a child: an anger that teaches them how to live in the world. "I do not need you to like me but for God's sake, be better than this tonight."

The Spitehouse is sprouting windows and stairs. Here is the piano room, the guest room, the living room, and the kitchen. Here is the room she grew up in and the room she has now been stashed in like an unsightly bit of furniture. Doors are the last thing to return; cleansing air and light pour through. Sometimes Calla thinks these periods of rebuilding are the only reason she plays the game. The dream that you might go again and again to the selfsame state of the world. "What's the matter, Rodge? Worried I'll wake the ghosts?"

"Your sister and I have tried to take care of you. We've given you money, connections, shelter, education—"

"How very fatherly of you."

"—and we have demanded nothing in return. Do you realize that? Do you realize how generous that is? Do you think every girl who comes out of Tisch with a song in her heart and too much Eugene O'Neill on her shelves gets the same?"

Calla says, "That money belongs to the family."

Here is the crux. Roger doesn't know how he could have missed it. It is like a headline printed on the night. Sad, little Calla St. Cloud, fed up with writing domestic dramas, comes home seeking a life of ease. She wants only to languish on chaises longues and snack on bonbons and finally read Proust so she can stop lying in interviews about having done so. Well. It will be easy to get rid of her. Come morning he'll pull out the checkbook, give her a little patrician (*not* fatherly!) speech, and she'll be on her way.

Roger has won but is too much the gamesman to smirk. "In the fair eyes of spirits, that may be true, Calla. But in the eye of the law, the money is your sister's." Roger knows that he will always win; he bears none of the St. Cloud family sins. But Calla goes down swinging.

"Maybe you killed them, Rodge," she says. "Maybe you were the voice in the walls. How much does a true-crime book pay, anyway? Maybe I'll try my hand at writing one."

Now halfway out the room, he says, "See you later, Calla. So good to have you home." The door closes behind him.

The Spitehouse's regeneration completes. Calla's spindly avatar descends to the basement. As empty as the upper floors except for this: a vault door where no vault door should be. She didn't place it there and cannot open it. Flames don't touch it. She rises, locks her bedroom door, and resumes her game.

FIVE

THE MASTER BEDROOM, like its four-poster bed, has held three generations of St. Clouds. Two planed Craftsman dressers hide six decades of dust in their joints. On warm days, Edna still catches her mother's faint baby-powder scent. Edna's chief additions are lamps: a white gooseneck desk lamp, a wrought-iron floor lamp, an extendable light bolted to the wall over an armchair so that Roger has a place to read at night. Beyond these, the walls are decked with acquaintances' photos—grain silos and gas stations—and a watercolor of the American desert. There's a shot of her and Roger outside the courthouse on their wedding day. It was October; she wore a white sheath dress and a veil they'd bought at a costume shop.

Edna often thinks about that night in '92 in the rhythms of a children's poem: *For want of a nail, the shoe was lost. For want of a shoe, the horse was lost.* Cascading effect and cause. For want, for want. But after the ritual that for-want feeling fades. There is evil in the world. There are monsters in the dark. All you can do is survive.

She and Wren sort through a blue thirty-gallon Rubbermaid container of clothes—Edna's from when she was Wren's age. Proof, beyond the stories and photographs and movies Wren has grown up with, that a lost world lingers in something she can touch.

In the corner: the watchful eye of Edna's camera; its spindly tripod legs.

Wren tugs out a tattered pair of low-rise jeans. "Cripes, these are hideous."

"Your clothes will be hideous, too, in nineteen years."

"That doesn't mean anything to me, Mom. I can't conceive of more years than I've been alive."

"Maybe you can't, little bird, but some of us have to try."

There are so *many* clothes here. Dresses and plaid skirts and *a Simpsons T-shirt?* Edna can't imagine why she saved them all. She wears a yearlong uniform of black jeans and a black cotton top—tank, tee, or long-sleeve, ebbing with the season. These clothes spark no recognition as Wren stacks them neatly by the tub. The connecting thread was cut years ago.

"How was it for you?" Edna asks. "The performance tonight."

"Wonderful."

"You say that as if you mean it."

"I mean it in the old sense: wonderful, awful, terrific." Wren has been attending the ritual since she was five, been carrying Edna's candle—by her own request—since she was eight. "It's a nightmare every year, but it has a nightmare's shocking beauty. A beauty we all share."

It fills Edna with the electric warmth of pleasure and pride—to have raised a daughter who thinks this carefully. If only thinking could protect her, out in the world.

Still. A nightmare. "Oh, love, I don't mean it to be."

"Of course you do. It needs to be a nightmare, don't you think?" She holds a silver slip dress over her body, measuring it against her. "Now this I love."

"Hold there, will you?"

Edna lines up the camera. Wren is practiced at holding still. The camera snaps.

"Not the right lighting," Edna says. "Hold on."

Lamps are rearranged. The gooseneck's turn shadows half of Wren's face. The dress's silver gleams. Everything sharpens. Again, the camera snap. "Now turn slightly toward me. There, that's good."

Snap.

Wren keeps her tone neutral when she asks, "Do you think these will be good enough for your next show?"

"Unimportant." But Edna had the same thought. What if she re-created those hospital self-portraits that made her famous: the stitches, the hollow look, the bruises and clinical absence of blood. Was there a nontrite way to do it, a real story to tell? "What would people think?"

"They'd say, 'In this brave new work, featuring her daughter—the spitting image of St. Cloud's youth—Edna St. Cloud returns to a quote, unquote, *simpler* time. A time before the traumas that haunted her early work.'"

Edna laughs. It was a stupid idea. "Go on," she says. Wren slips her arms into a flannel shirt, a pair of overalls. They hang limply over her like an apron. *Snap*. Wren turns her back—*snap*—and looks over her shoulder—*snap, snap*—and again faces the wall.

"'There is, in these photos, a longing for the time when *history was over*. A time that predates common mass killings. A time before so-called capital-*T* Terror demanded we go to war with it. And in projecting her own daughter backward into this fantasy past, we can read St. Cloud's ecstasies and agonies over her legacy and future.'" Edna is glad her daughter cannot see her wince.

"You've been spending too much time with your father."

Wren turns back. "I spend the exact correct amount of time with you both." She slips her hands into the overall pockets. "Can I have these?"

"Not so wretched now."

"You win, you win."

What a life Edna has. This too-clever daughter. This house. Books of her photographs on shelves across America. Roger—maddeningly opaque sometimes and yet, there he was, ever there, every night. It was as good a life as anyone got. What a shame, then, the cost.

She's been woken at night by thoughts of that plastered-over room. The paint has aged to match the walls. What if she forgets it's there? What if she drops her guard? But there is safety so long as everyone remains within shouting distance, and the candle burns through the night. Tomorrow will begin another year of freedom.

"Mom, is everything okay?"

Edna lines up her camera again. The photo, when developed, will show Wren looking serious, and scared, and older than fifteen.

"Nothing can hurt us, little bird."

"But there are lots of ways to hurt and be hurt, aren't there?"

"There are." Another snap. In this photo, Wren's expression will blur. "And none of them apply here."

"Is another gallery going to start selling your photos?"

Edna looks up from her camera. "Is that what you're worried about?"

"I'm worried about you being—"

"Because you know there's plenty of money."

"—unhappy."

"I don't need to sell photographs to be happy." Edna will tell herself this until it's true. There is the house, and Roger, and the candle. There is her daughter, who saved her from a life of pain and misery.

"But how can they drop you?" Wren says. "Don't they know who you are?"

"Everyone knows who I am. That's the problem."

"They must be idiots."

Edna laughs, the camera snaps. In this one, Wren will look exactly like the child she is.

"They are idiots," Edna says. "They're misogynists, capitalists, businessmen. They'd as soon be fishmongers as art dealers, if that would make them money. At least fish gets eaten, or rots, and people come back for more. With art, what you have is all you ever get." *Snap*. "There's nothing quite so easy to exploit as people's morbid curiosity. A murderer could make a fortune if he took before-and-afters of his victims."

"But that's not why you took those self-portraits in the hospital."

"No, love." The pictures were easy—to take, to consume. They were *immediate* and *raw* and *powerful*—words that made Edna feel like some kind of exotic tartare. She had tried to make something else—to use the blurring, blending possibility space of the medium, to represent nothing, only a record of light and shadow—and had reached the limits of the art world's patience. They wanted to consume every bit of her (the self-portraits, and her series of the house's empty hallways, her parents and husband, the fucking meals they shared); now that nothing's left, they're happy to spit back her bones. Maybe she never should have taken those hospital photos.

But imagine you find yourself in a hospital bed, barely remembering. It was a bad dream. A misunderstanding between flesh and knife. The real world was never like this. No danger could come between past and present tenses. You were safe. You are safe. And so, at day's end, when you're left all alone, you try to remember and forget at once. What else is there to do? Your parents left your camera; they never bothered to imagine a salvation but art and love. You shuffle to the bathroom, frame your face in the mirror.

There's a bruise under your cheek. There, when you pull away your droopy gown, is the stitching's brutal centipede. There is something in your eyes: a reflection of a reflection. A picture of a picture. And you think that, if the Victorians were right that the eye recorded one's last sight before death, their graveyards would have been like photo albums. And you don't want to lose the moment. You want proof—for yourself, for everyone—of who you are and what you've done and what's been done to you.

This is what she has tried to teach Wren. This she remembers each time the viewfinder comes between her and the world. There is life and there is its image and you need distance between them.

Edna's camera clicks impotently. "Look at that," she says. "All out of film."

SIX

ROGER WAITS OUT the night in his study. Around him is a profusion of papers, awards, ornaments. There are hundreds of books—his own work, and background research, and the Victorians he read in the small Ohio library of his youth. He holds a corded phone, his private line, to his ear. With his free hand, he flips again through the book that remains his bestselling: *Doll Parts: Isolation, Transvestism, and the St. Cloud Family Murders*. He always returns to it on this night. He will never forget what it was like to be twenty-seven—with only his microcassette recorder, a stack of mimeographed police files, and that beautiful, fierce girl on the other side of the table. The electricity between them. This was real writing. In the seventeen years and four books since, he's never again reached such heights.

Into the phone, he says, "Let's go back to the summer of '07, shall we? Your mother said she was traveling for work. How long was she gone for?"

On the phone's far end, Diana Cutter—his latest beautiful, fierce girl—is articulate and energetic. She is twenty-five and on Pacific time. Roger's pen scratches *X*'s and *O*'s in the old book's margins, a gridless tic-tac-toeing. A watchful ghost might think he wasn't listening at all.

"Which is when she showed you the gun," he says.

It was perhaps inevitable, he reads, *that in the first days of Roland St. Cloud's infamy, the usual suspects were eager to blame Satanism, heavy metal music, pornography, etc. Less remarked on was the apparent lack of origin point for Roland's flavor of the occult. A quick study of his library checkouts offered no dour or foreboding texts—nothing more arcane and mysterious than the collected Blake. Though it's been some years since I read "Jerusalem," I believe I'd recall if it were packed with magical spells by which a boy might transform his body into a girl's.*

"People have suggested," Roger says into the phone, "that there's no way she could have driven to the suburbs of Chicago and back in time for your graduation." He is a professional; he modulates, shies off from easy answers. "Diana, if we do not address all the exotic theorizing that armchair criminologists get up to we—" Her admonition comes shorter, louder now. "Yes, of *course* I'm writing down what you say."

Doll Parts continues: *Rather, what's clear in the pages of Roland St. Cloud's diary is how little guidance he had. Careful students of transvestism's history may have expected an encounter with his forebears—Einar Wegener and George Jorgensen both published memoirs in the early part of this century—but there is no reference to their names, nor any clue that he thought his problem historically precedented.*

"This is our chance to clear up any misconception," Roger says. "You understand that, don't you? This is our best opportunity to take control of the narrative."

Perhaps he was too embarrassed to ask for such a book. Perhaps he did ask and did not like what he found. It does not take a history student to imagine the difficulty with which these men lived. Better to go beyond cross-dressing. Better to shed the masculine shell and take on the body that you believe—by rights—ought to have been yours.

"One of the most prolific female serial killers in American history—naturally people will suggest she did not act alone. This is a story about evils that women are no less capable of than men."

A joke is made, and Roger laughs.

"No, *not* like Edna. Naughty girl."

He checks the door—closed—and returns to his book.

Roland St. Cloud's obscure symbology—the spirals and stars that littered his diaries, the crosses that marred his victims' bodies—did not come from the Church of Satan or Aleister Crowley, Slayer or Blake. His diagrams, his spells, his whole uncommon ritual began firmly in the decaying palace of his mind.

"Now, the graduation. The heart was still warm, roasting in the trunk of her car."

A question.

"Oh, it's fine," he says. "Much the same as always."

Any crime, any act at all, could be written about badly or well. But *Doll Parts* had been a romantic act. Proof to Edna in the wake of their wakeful nights that he was not only the man who would love her best but the narrator laureate of her traumas.

"You know I can't think about that right now," he tells Diana. And then, glancing at the door, whispers: "I miss you too."

Telling anyone's story is an act of either love or cruelty.

"Soon, love. Soon."

It was necessary to get creative here and there. Embellish, to shore up the cracks. Edna understood it all sounded like conjecture otherwise. What did it matter if Roland never kept a diary? Roger understood the boy well enough to invent one, to generate sentences Roland might have written. Sentences that were true insofar as they captured his soul. Verifying how strange, verging on inexplicable, the entire affair was.

The trick was to get the survivors—the work's true subject—to understand the narrative demands. If you could tell them a story about their lives so convincing that they, too, believed it, your work was done.

"Of course her rituals are silly," he says. "They're *rituals*. No sillier than the way you sit by the door for thirty seconds before you go on a trip. Or my writing notes with the pen you gave me." A golden flash as the pen twirls in his fingers. "That's the nature of ritual: it's all in the act. *The means by which the unconscious mind communicates with the conscious*, Jung said."

Hemming and hawing from Diana. She's smart—a political theory PhD at Berkeley. She can identify each of Shostakovich's symphonies within a few bars. She has her own ideas about stories, and this is why the new book is going so slowly. If only he could spend more time . . .

"Of course. Of course I love—"

A knock at the door cuts short speech and thought.

"Come in!"

Heather enters, still in her pajamas. "I figured it would be locked," she says.

Roger holds up a finger for pause. "All right, Ms. Cutter. Yes. Yes. I'll be in touch in the morning. Good evening, Ms. Cutter." And hangs up.

"Sorry to interrupt."

"Nonsense, Heather, nonsense. Please come in, sit down."

Heather doesn't. The study's mess of piles is unlike the rigid order of every other room. No surface uncovered, including the chairs.

Roger is pleased that she's come to see him. He admires that Heather does not shy from the St. Cloud family tragedies. He anticipates future meetings, wisdom he might share, and commiseration. To love a St. Cloud, he will say, is to hitch your carriage to a team of capricious horses. You will be tugged into the ditches as often as you are carried home. You will forever be kept at a distance by the same straps and buckles that keep them close.

She says, "That was Diana Cutter?"

"What? Oh, yes. Still awake out in California, you know."

"I heard about it on the news."

Annabeth Cutter's face beamed out from every grocery tabloid rack. Pretty and young for fifty-three. A face half the world wanted to kill and half wanted to fuck.

"Terrible, what happened," Roger says. "The father's been out of the picture for quite some while; Diana and her mother were always very close. To discover the person you loved most, the person who raised and protected you all your life, had killed at least fifteen people in cold blood . . . it makes this family's business seem, I don't know, rather small."

"Oh. Um, I guess."

"What's your James up to this evening?"

"He's watching that movie," Heather says.

"Ah, yes. I believe watching *Dollmaker* is *his* ritual. Funny movie, isn't it?"

"Funny?"

"I would have liked it if a young Robert Redford could play my role. I suppose we rarely get stories told the way we'd want. Only in a handful of scenes, anyway."

A team of capricious horses, he writes in the margins. *The libidinal urge vis-à-vis murder. Morts, petite and grande*. Heather does not relax while he writes. Surely she would not confuse his scratchings—his *X*'s and *O*'s and orgasmic meditations—for a besotted child's love notes. Ridiculous. He shuts the book and pockets the pen.

"Roger."

"Heather."

"I wanted to ask. I mean." She fears she's betraying James by being here. "What made Roland hurt those women? I don't mean what he wanted but—what happened to him? What was his life like before?"

"Oh, surely James could tell—"

"No," Heather says, too fast. "I mean, he doesn't really remember anything." She loves James—no matter if he goes about each day in a haze. No matter if he barely notices when she touches him. And the skirt—

Roger says, "Well, Roland felt 'like the smallest Russian doll buried in a plastic Easter egg.' So his diary reported, at least." He was still proud of that metaphor.

"But lots of people are confused about their gender and they don't kill people."

"You and I have known each other for four years, Heather. If there's something you need to ask, please ask it."

Heather has always loved boys. The sweaty tang on the back of their necks, the flat, hard expanse of their chests. She loves the way James's cock feels when they have sex, hooked to something deep and ancient inside her. There's nothing that can undo her love for him. But love is not the only thing.

Roger is the safest person for her to talk to. It's not like he pays attention. He had not heard her approach—had no clue she'd been listening at his office door.

"Could anyone have known?" Heather asks. "About Roland's condition, I mean."

"If he'd wanted help, then yes, perhaps."

"Help?"

"There are tests, you know, to ensure it's more than a whim. There are hormones and surgery. It's a bit like training a method actor." Roger rubs his eyes. Already he misses Diana's voice. The soft flesh of her thigh and the places her cheekbones catch the light. He wants to talk about her killer mother's hands. It is late, and the night has hours yet to run. "The trouble, in fact, is that it's so much like method acting. If you're a man, you can only pretend at womanhood. A sort of mask the transvestite wears over his true face. And I don't believe Roland St. Cloud would have been satisfied with a mask. It was the doll's life he wanted: a womanhood that's solid all the way through."

"But what did that *feel* like?" Had Roland also had these hazy days? Did he recoil at the touch of love? What good is having this house, this ritual, this book, if no one can tell her?

"Roland was jealous of his sister," Roger says. "Outraged that he couldn't have the life she'd been given, any more than I could make Robert Redford young in 1995. Time only turns one way. Why do you ask all this?"

"I've been thinking about the ritual, is all," she says.

"Ah yes, the repetition of the act, if only in acting. It sticks in your head."

She has never truly entered the room. Only hung between Roger and the closed door.

Heather points at the copy of *Doll Parts* on his desk. "Were you reading to prepare for tonight?"

"Yes and no."

"Would you mind if I borrowed it?"

He offers it up. "You've read it before, of course."

"Yeah. Time for a reread, is all."

"Certainly, certainly." Thank God this conversation is coming to an end. "Never fear, Heather. The circumstances that created Roland St. Cloud are as singular as his particular crimes. No matter how many of those *Dollmaker* movies they make."

SEVEN

CALLA SITS WITH her back to the room as she plays her game. Her avatar waits in the Spitehouse, mute but for the sound of synthesized wind.

The Neighborhood's 16-bit graphics and gameplay are common enough among simulation games. But the innovations of its creator (a Dutch national, or Swedish, depending on whose reports you believed) were enormous. Each user's computer is employed as a server, hosting a procedurally generated scrap of digital world—land on which they can build a house, or a shop, or a grotesque kinetic sculpture of metal and meat. You can manufacture jewelry, feasts, mid-century modern furniture. Other players can visit, buy up new land, sell resources or mineral rights or folktales. Or you can dig down until you hit mantle and your character dies.

The game is unwieldy, random, imprecise. It is like an endless forest, new life ever waiting in the dark. It invents animals, landscapes, stars, events. Rumor was that a UFO had crash-landed in one person's backyard; whatever came out of it vanished without a trace. Rumor was a pop star had gotten her latest hit melody from an in-game choir of frogs. Rumor was there was a house-size plum that granted wishes. There were too many rumors for all to be true, but they couldn't all be false. There is the vault, after all. If Calla sits still, and waits long enough, there will be more mysteries, more answers.

Wren says, "That looks an awful lot like—"

"Ohjesusgoddammntittyfuckingchrist." Calla is out of her seat at the first syllable.

"—sorry—our house."

"Does nobody knock anymore?"

"The door's open."

Surely Calla's body does not need to maintain this state of panic. The maniac breaths, worry vibrating in her fingertips. She sits to hide her shaking. Her index finger twitches on the mouse.

Calla says, "You've been behind me how long?"

"Is that *The Neighborhood*?"

"What do you know about *The Neighborhood*?"

"It's supposed to have been created by some agoraphobic genius. People play it instead of living real life."

"And do you think that's what I'm doing?"

"No," Wren says. "You live in New York. Your whole life is unreal."

"Oh cute, she thinks she knows things."

Wren is unbothered by this third-person dismissal. Her aunt was popular when she was a teen, which makes your personality calcify. Calla is no different from those middle school mean girls.

"That's our house," Wren reiterates. "You're in my bedroom."

"*Our* nothing. You and I own this house as much as the squirrels do."

"Why's your avatar look like a hand made out of needles?"

"Have you played?"

"No," Wren says. "I mostly play stuff like *Colossal Cave Adventure*."

Of course she does. Roger should be jailed for raising a child so ill-suited to modern life.

"Well, maybe by the time you're my age you'll find there've been new games since the seventies."

"You know *Adventure*?"

"Look," Calla says. "Here we are in the basement. A perfect reproduction except—"

"What is that? A bank vault? Why'd you put that—"

"I didn't." Calla's avatar whacks the vault door with a sledge-hammer. A tinny cartoon *ding* comes from the speakers at each strike. "I built the house and the vault grew like a mushroom."

"So how do you open it?"

"I don't know. Watch this."

Again into her inventory. Again with the matches. The house should be used to this. It should be groaning: *Here we go again*. Pixelated flames spread from room to room.

There's no surprise in Wren's voice. "What'd you do that for?"

"I'll bring it back."

There is a digital flicker across their faces. It's comforting—like a real fire on Christmas Eve. When the house is no more, the vault door shines proudly in the middle of its charred and ashen field.

"Indestructible," Wren says. "As any vault worth its bank would be."

"A permanent thing. A still point in the turning world."

"I'm not sure that's what Eliot meant."

Calla's pleased. "She knows Eliot."

"Things you'd know, Auntie Calla, if you ever came home."

That breaks it.

"Yes, well, I really *have* missed out, haven't I?" Calla says. "Teenagers quoting modernists and playing fucking *Adventure*. You probably own a muff too. You'll probably catch consumption in some Alpine lodge. Is this what teenagers are like nowadays?"

"I have no idea what teenagers are like. I don't go to school anymore."

"Oh God, I'm sure that father of yours hired you a fucking *governess*. It's probably his wet dream to give his daughter a Victorian childhood. He's like a fundamentalist Christian, you know, only his Bible is *Bleak House*."

The gravity of this room, the whole house, shifts with Calla here. It is morally neutral, Wren thinks. Only different.

"Why are you here," Wren asks, "now?"

"She nags and then complains."

"I'm only asking."

"I've stopped writing."

A pause. In this family, to cease making art is tantamount to dying.

"You know," Wren says, "when my dad has writer's block I sometimes read—"

"Did I say writer's block?" Calla clicks around. Each piece of the Spitehouse snaps again into place. It is the moment of a dive before hitting cool, clear chlorine. "I can write. I can produce gunk like a clogged drain. I don't want to."

"Why not?"

"It doesn't make anything happen."

"Auden—"

"Enough."

"But isn't that—"

"If you say 'the point' so help me God."

"—proven false by your entire life?"

Calla wants to burn the house down again. She would banish Wren if she could bear the thought of what this obnoxious girl-pixie must have done to her childhood room.

"What *ever* could you mean by that, Wren?"

"My father literally wrote the book on your family—"

"Your father wrote a book about roughly thirty minutes of my family's long and storied history—"

"—though I guess you were pretty much absent for all of it."

"—which was then turned into a bargain-bin *Silence of the Lambs* knockoff—"

"Not to mention you took up the mantle of your playwright parents, yielding your own moderate success."

"Hang on. Who called my success 'moderate'?"

"The *New York Times*."

That must have come after she'd stopped paying attention.

"The point is," Wren says, "writing built this house. It made this family what it is today. You can call that a shallow consequence if you like, but it's an object reminder that—"

"Is that where you think all this comes from?"

Wren, for the first time tonight, doesn't know what to think. Where else, after all? And what was the point of all those killings, if not to raise the St. Clouds to a visible height?

She says, "I mean, there's some meager inheritance."

"Which came from . . . ?"

"Well, as I said, Grandma and Grandpa were—"

"Do you really not know or are you being intentionally dense?"

It was foolish of Calla to think Edna ever would tell her daughter. Twice foolish to have stayed away so long, depriving her dear niece of this knowledge.

"Stop treating me like a child," Wren says.

"By the sound of it, I'm the only person in this house treating you like an adult. Sit down." Wren falls into the leather armchair. Picks at its peeling patches. "What do you know about your great-grandfather?"

"Practically nothing."

"Grandad St. Cloud—my father's father—inherited a petroleum concern down in Louisiana when his own father died, at age forty-five, of a heart attack. St. Cloud Petrochem had been limping along for some decades in a feeble attempt to compete with Vaseline." Calla's own parents hadn't been forthcoming about the family legacy either. Only by chasing down a footnote in one of her high school history books had she learned any of this. "When his father died, the business was on the brink of failure. Grandad felt certain there were other uses for their products. He pitched them as everything from engine lubricant to appetite suppressant."

Wren says nothing. She is not used to not knowing.

"When the war effort began in the thirties, there was pressure on every domestic industry to assist with the anti-Axis cause. It was then that he began experimenting with weapons applications for petroleum jelly."

"You're telling me he, what, invented napalm?"

"Ultimately, no. His experiments with magnesium burned too fast to do any real harm." One more near miss in the St. Cloud family history. "But he developed methods for gelling petroleum cheaply at scale. He had a few big demonstrations for Uncle Sam, made some connections at the War Department. All of which led to a big, fat weapons contract for St. Cloud Petrochem." Calla can't help herself. Their legacy is the beauty of a derailed train. This is the hurt, the curse, the world turns back on them.

"It was St. Cloud fire that destroyed Tokyo and Dresden," she says. "It was St. Cloud fire that burned innocent, citizen flesh. It was the same fire that filled flamethrowers in the Korean and Vietnam Wars. That's the thing about fire, dear niece: the more it burns, the more it wants."

"You're very obviously making this up." Wren thinks of the digital house on fire. The parade of images Calla conjures to hurt her.

"Oh?"

"If we were, I don't know, getting checks from the Department of Defense I feel like I would know."

"You *feel like*?"

"Shut up."

"This is what it means to be an adult, Wren. To be trusted with difficult information. To look at the horror of our history in its face."

"You're saying this to hurt me, and I won't let it."

It better hurt her, Calla thinks. Let those wounds bleed until they scar. That's the only way to survive this family.

"Well, you're right about the checks. After Korea, Grandad sold his shares. I believe he spent the rest of his short life learning Appalachian folk songs."

Wren says, "The money must have run out ages ago."

"And what if it did? It was that money that built this house and staged our parents' silly little plays. It was that money that funded the ridiculous film my brother is so fond of watching—the one you think keeps this family afloat. You've gotten every bit of it backward."

A silence follows.

"You wanted to be a writer, didn't you?" Calla cannot stop now. "You wanted to be like your daddy. Like your big aunt Calla. Well, I'm here to disabuse you. Art is a shell game. The stuff that makes the world move is capital—war and capital. You keep that in mind fifty years from now when your children's children ask why the world is on fire. You tell them it's so we could all keep our little hobbies. Tell them proudly that that's their great-great-great-grandaddy's fire. Tell them, *Be grateful for the warmth.* Tell them, *That's family*."

Calla isn't lying. She means it when she says she treats Wren as an adult. But there's a difference between telling the truth and being right. Wren says, "You're wrong."

"You know I'm not."

"The obvious truth," Wren says, "is that you failed. Maybe you wrote plays because you were good at it and maybe you did it to remember your parents. But either way, you didn't get enough from it. Don't make that my problem.

"People are always telling me that in a few years I'll leave this place," Wren goes on. "I'll go out and see what the world is really like. But I can't see what I'd do that for. Look at you, gone and back again. You came limping home with nothing in your hands. Now you're stuck here like the rest of us. And not even in your own bedroom."

EIGHT

THIS VERSION OF Bea smokes on the porch swing. This version of Edna bums a cigarette, lights it, doesn't breathe. They drift through late May's tree-frog song. *One day*, Bea says, *we'll go somewhere far away from here.*

Yeah right. We'll be lucky if we get as far as UVA. Edna's face is softened by time and cheap film stock.

I mean it. Bea pries away the cigarette and brings it to Edna's lips. Edna sucks in, takes back the cig, exhales. *One day*, Bea says, *I'm gonna hop in my car and drive west and keep driving. I'm going to hit the ocean going so fast I'm gonna skip across it.*

Edna laughs. *Just watch. We're going to be two old hags with a gaggle of brats playing in the sprinkler while we sit on this exact porch and smoke Parliament fucking Lights.*

Bea scrunches her face in disgust, opens her mouth to speak. From deep inside the house comes Vera's scream. James hits the pause button, and both girls freeze.

It's a strong choice, *Dollmaker* not showing Vera's death. We see Polly stabbed in the half-lit bathroom—but Roland is a blur. We know he's the killer; we have seen him prepare his body, anoint himself in clownish makeup. But the moment of final reveal is withheld.

James can hear every step in the house. Wren's confident tread in the kitchen, followed by Edna's light, tentative steps. Muffled voices and the microwave's beep and the creak in the third step as Wren returns upstairs. Heather hasn't come back from Roger's study. Decompressing after the ritual, probably, with the only other outsider. James hadn't bothered to tell her: Roger's as inside as any of them.

Or else. James doesn't like to think—*Is this normal? Is my boyfriend a fag? How do I get out of this?*—what she's saying. Again he worries his brother's puzzle box; again he fails to open it. Rewinds the film. Bea's voice again: *I'm going to hit the ocean going so fast I'm gonna skip across it.* Pause. You could hold them here forever. A dream that doesn't end.

There was a time James wanted to be a screenwriter. To propagate these nightmares, create a killer that might be talked about in slumber-party bedrooms all across America. It had taken until he was twelve, and his parents finally let him watch *Dollmaker*, that he understood there was no point. The monster was already here.

He thinks of David Cronenberg's VHS prophet: *Whatever appears on the television screen emerges as raw experience for those who watch it. Therefore, television is reality . . .*

One of these days he's going to write an essay about *Dollmaker* and all its off-kilter knockoffs. He'll domesticate it through analysis. Separate it from himself. Suddenly it's only a movie, not the story of his life. Sometimes, working at the video store, he makes notes on scraps of receipt paper. He burns them in the employee bathroom before going home.

Not including the five sequels, there are at least two dozen movies piggybacking on *Dollmaker*'s success. Though it exists in a lineage with *Psycho*, and *Sleepaway Camp*, and *The Silence of the Lambs*, it was this scrappy little 1995 production—made at the edge of the teen slasher's heyday—that gave rise to the modern transsexual slasher.

The thing that separates *Dollmaker* and its progeny from earlier films is the director's choice not to disguise his cross-dressing killer. The case was high profile. We know from the outset that it's the St. Cloud brother who will kill. We know the names of his victims.

Instead of relishing the mystery, *Dollmaker* focuses on the normal, easy lives of its victims and the killer's inability to make the same for himself. We watch him slip into tights that bag around his narrow thighs and flat ass. We watch him paste makeup over his eyes and lips. He paints his nails singing along to Shirley Bassey's "I (Who Have Nothing)" in a warbly basso. Before he leaves the bathroom, he wipes this secret face away. An ugly clump of nail polish—missed by the acetone pad—clings to his nail bed, and at school, Bea Fulton teases him for it. The film asks for our pity even as the camera gives up following him. Instead, it trails Bea to her history class, where she slides into her desk and proclaims to her best friend, *That brother of yours is such a fag.*

Pick any of the film's descendants, James would say—2001's *Can I Spend the Night?*, 1998's *Alone*, 2005's *Summer Loving*. In each, we see a similar sequence of the killer failing to prepare himself. These are men who try on the costume of womanhood and, finding it insufficient, resort to violence. Each made monstrous by their failures of masculinity as Freddy Krueger is by his burn marks. But unlike Freddy, these men can disguise their monstrosity behind their everyday faces. To pass, out in the world, as—if not a normal man, at least a man who knows he is one.

These are slashers that, as Carol J. Clover writes, collapse *the categories masculine and feminine . . . into the same character.* But unlike Buffalo Bill or Norman Bates, these killers do not hide away in obscure retreats. They attempt to live in the world—as projectionists and bartenders, as boyfriends and brothers. Revelation comes when they can no longer contain their monstrosity. They stalk out into the night with their faces painted. They bare themselves to the world—blouses ripped, dresses wriggled out of. Their flat, hairy chests and limp pricks; the very fact of their maleness bared to the night and to their victims.

It's this that *Dollmaker*'s Roland shares with his descendants, James thinks. Not his madness, not his murders, but his plain-faced inability to *be*.

GOD, WHAT IS taking Heather? Of course they'll have to talk about it, and of course it'll be tonight.

These are the times that James most misses his parents. They were dead by Thanksgiving of his freshman year of college. He never got a chance to talk through heartbreak. Never got to reach an equal understanding of the world. To sit on the couch between the people who reared him from a little slug of a baby to a full human being. At the time they died they still thought of him as the sweet and nervous one whose favorite movie was *Abbott and Costello Meet Frankenstein*. After his father's mind started to go, the times James visited, there was hardly any history to forget. He was a child then. Who might he have become if not for their loss?

In the hallway outside his room, he stands before the blank section of wall where there was once a door. James comes here sometimes in dreams. Roland is trapped and running out of breath; there is the crack of a neck breaking; there is a tornado that splinters his dolls.

James wishes he could ask his parents about opening the room. Air it out, repaint the walls. Make it into something—anything—else. But the house is Edna's now, and she would never. It isn't covered up so that they'll forget. No one in this family can forget.

By sealing it away, they go on remembering. Ensure that it will never be *just another room*. James can feel breath leaking out of him. On the far side of the house, Heather laughs.

Fuck it. He doesn't have to wait around. He knocks twice on the wall—as if to prove that there is no one behind it—and descends into the closed-off puzzle box of the St. Cloud family home.

NINE

PLENTY IN THE kitchen has changed or been replaced over the years. The fridge is only five years old, the oven even newer. Scorched copper-bottom pans have been swapped for untarnished steel. But the kitchen table is the butter-colored Formica one the St. Clouds grew up with. Incongruously shabby and irreplaceable. There's a splotchy stain from an ill-fated pasta dish; a black mark on the rim where Calla, practicing a monologue for the family, stubbed out a cigarette. When the table's moved, twice a year, to clean beneath, there are four clear divots where its legs rest.

It's there the ritual candle burns. It has hours left to go.

It's there that Edna sits with the catalog from her very first show. She called it *Renaissance*, a kind of joke. But there is something fancifully italic in the sprawled, hospital bed self-portraits. Thin blanket barely covering her scarred and bandaged chest. *I woke in the same hospital in which I was born*, she wrote in her artist's statement. *Born for a second time. Not as a twin, but as the eldest daughter. Not as a girl, but as an adult with all the burden of the world's horrors. We were a family of one fewer from then on. It was in these images that I came to understand that.*

When she met Roland at the top of the basement steps, it was like they'd made a trade. He in her makeup, her dress; she with the knife he'd taken from the kitchen. And for a moment she thought: Is this who I am too? Is this the closeness of twinship? But that worry did not keep her from stabbing him. She went to the hospital, he went to the psych ward, and she forgot the feeling.

James enters, humming Shirley Bassey. For years Edna has gotten that song stuck in her head. Lying in the tub, or waiting in the hotel lobby for Roger to check out. It was stuck in her head before she went under for her C-section. *I can only watch you with my nose pressed up against the windowpane. I, I who have nothing.*

"Hello, Eddie." A mad bounce in his step as he hums his way to the fridge. He fills a tall glass with milk and drains it in one go. Refills the glass, replaces the carton. James never feels more like a boy than in this house. He could be eighteen and home from college. What life might have been. "Looking at photos of yourself?"

"I'm not taking criticism from a grown man drinking milk."

"Who's criticizing?"

"How's your movie?" Edna asks.

"Same as always."

"You had a crush on the girl playing me, if I recall."

"Everyone had a crush on her." James sips his milk. "This place would feel less sepulchral if you guys got a cat again."

"*Sepulchral?*"

"It's been, what, three years since the Grampus died?"

"Two." The Grampus was a gargantuan, gray tabby stray who adopted the St. Cloud–Merrilows in his old age. A bit of Fancy Feast, shelter from the summer storms. He came and went as he pleased, slept in a living room chair. They'd tried to keep him inside toward the end, but he yowled at the door for hours. Christ, the *lungs* on that cat.

Edna loved him, though. The sun on his belly, his chin in her hand. Purr like an oil-hungry lawn mower. Edna could spend an hour watching him watch birds out the window. He hadn't needed the St. Clouds, had chosen them even so. It was Edna who found him in the early morning, cold in his living room chair. She'd thrown open the doors as though to release his soul, to let him out into the bright and bird-filled day one final time. She buried him in the yard, in the shadow of a willow oak.

James says, "You go to Starkweather yesterday?"

"Same as always."

"How is he?"

"Alive, unfortunately." If you call that hollow-eyed disregard living.

"Guess he still isn't speaking."

"No," Edna says.

"So you, what, sit there and look at each other? 'Well, it's been another year.'"

"I look him in the eyes and I say, 'You're never going to kill me.'"

"That's not fair, Eddie. He never actually wanted to kill you."

"That's pretty much academic, don't you think?"

In the photobook: Edna in black and white, an ashen confetti of petals across her gown. Her stitches tore open when she stood to adjust the camera.

"Does he know about the movie?" James asks.

"Only if you told him."

"I don't tell him anything."

Edna closes the book. It's proof of the ritual's power, James thinks, that she is looking at these photos tonight. That she sits with her back to the kitchen windows. "You loved him," she says. "As much—more—than any of us."

"I was six."

"You were his favorite."

"What am I going to say? 'Hey, bro, I know you don't recognize me, but pretend I'm you. Living the life you never got to.'"

"Don't tease, Jamie. What would you actually say?"

"Oh, uh." He gulps milk. When he visits Roland, it's not like he keeps silent. He talks about the sound of wind through the trees. The family of rabbits living behind his duplex. It's the chaff of daily living he wants to offer. Birds migrating down from Canada. Roadwork on his commute. All the human things his brother will never get.

James says, "I'd tell him I work in a video store. I'd say, 'I remember going to Blockbuster as kids, and you'd walk me down the horror aisle because I was too scared to go alone. We'd make up plots based on the title and the poster. *Halloween* was about a haunted rubber mask. *Candyman* was obviously about a beekeeper who turned people into living hives. *The Texas Chain Saw Massacre*, unfortunately, spoke for itself.'"

Candyman wouldn't have been at the store because it came out after the attacks. It was playing the first time she and Roger went out together. Too early, then, to call it a date.

"What else?" Edna asks.

"'My girlfriend, Heather, works at a bakery next to the video store. On our breaks we smoke in the parking lot and eat day-old Danishes.'"

"He'd like that. He'd be happy you're happy."

"Yeah."

A silence.

"It's such a relief you aren't an artist," Edna says. A gesture at the book. "You don't have to worry about any of this bullshit." And, before he can respond: "When are you going to ask Heather?"

He sputters, coughs, droplets of milk on the tablecloth. What did Eddie know? What did Heather—

"Jesus Christ, Jamie." Edna's up, thumping his back. "It isn't dramatic as all that." Red-faced, wheezing in time with her thumps. "You've been together four years, I'm sure she expects you'll get married."

Ah. Right. A rushed call home to confirm Heather's invitation. A confession—not that Edna would see it as one—that he would propose soon.

The coughing slows. "Soon," he rasps. "I think."

"You think?"

He gulps down more milk. One final cough. "Surely she gets a say in it as well."

"Who could say no to you?"

"If she makes it through tonight, we'll find out." Back on autopilot. He's James. The normal one. The least miserable among them.

"We love her, Jamie. Mom and Dad would, too, if—they were here." Edna settles into the candle flame's birthday light. "I can see her and Mom at the counter, kneading out dough. Seven of us gathered at the piano for Christmas. Dad playing those old Gershwin songs because he didn't know any Christmas carols."

"Eight of us."

"Hmm?"

"Eight of us with Calla. Nine, if she brought anyone."

"Calla would never."

He's *normal. He's* normal.

"Were we a happy family?" James asks. "Before, I mean."

Edna does not hesitate. There is a light in her eyes you'd think would never stop dancing.

"The happiest."

TEN

WREN'S AVATAR LOOKS like five wooden buckets, stacked in a homunculoid shape. Calla is in the peeling leather chair, coaching Wren through *The Neighborhood*. There is a plate of cooling onion rings beside her.

"Buy that guy's pickaxe," Calla instructs.

"Can't I make one?"

"You'd need one to mine ore, to smelt into bars, to craft another pickaxe."

"Sounds like a flaw in the system."

"How do you think the world works?"

The man hawking tools has a friendly face. Eyes lost in wrinkles, gray beard spilling down his flannel belly. There are no NPCs in *The Neighborhood*. Somewhere—in this city or across the world—someone sits at the computer and trades these things for digital gold.

The pickaxe is rusted and small in the grip of Wren's bucket golem. "It's stronger than it looks," Calla says. "You can use it to hack through most anything—dirt, walls."

"The vault?"

"She knows it isn't that easy."

Thanks! Wren types into the chat box. The words appear in phosphor green over her avatar's head.

You're welcome! the bearded man says. *Happy mining! Let me know if you want help finding an ore vein!*

"All right, head back to your place now," Calla says. Wren's house is a shack, a cot, an ugly square representing a hot plate. The windows don't have glass in them. Leaves blow through when the wind picks up. "Now you can start digging for ore and stone to upgrade your place." The thing most people don't understand about this game is that it isn't a retreat from the dailiness of life. The game itself *is* the dailiness. The screen darkens as Wren digs deeper.

"Back in New York," Calla says, "there was this movie I saw. *Movie* isn't the word—it's an art piece. A twenty-four-hour film montage of other films, all clips in which clocks appear. It's synced to the actual time, so when it's 6:03 P.M. in real life, you're seeing movie clips where it's also 6:03 P.M. This guy took me to the museum; there was a huge line of people waiting to get in. So we stand there for ages, nothing to do but stand. You can see the edges of other artwork in galleries branching off from the hall. And I think: This is what we're waiting for. Bliss seen from the shores of pleasure."

"Barthes," Wren says. She shouldn't care about impressing her aunt, but she rarely gets the chance to show off. In middle school, the other girls abducted her books and drowned them in toilet stalls. They'd push wet tissues and used pads through her locker door. It got worse when they figured out who she was—snickering in the halls over a copy of her dad's book. On Halloween they came dressed up as the girls: Edna, Beatrice, and the rest. And when Wren said, *You know they got killed, right?* they said, *Who's going to do the killing this time, freak? You?*

Calla goes on. "I pretend the waiting *is* the experience. The movie's called *The Clock*. The awareness of time passing. The slow slipping-away of grains of sand. I suggest a game to the guy—we'll write notes on scraps of paper and reverse pickpocket them into people's coats—but neither of us has a pen. Life is Purgatory.

"When we get into the screening room, it actually isn't like waiting in line at all. It's—sort of compelling. There isn't a narrative except for the accumulation of minutes into hours. But time itself is enough. There is the same suspense and surprise that any good film brings. What scene will the artist pull next? What will be revealed? An hour passes."

Wren's heard of *The Clock*. She reads *Artforum* like everyone else. But it must be nice to live somewhere such things are commonplace. Everyone you know coming out to the museum, chatting with your friends in line. Having friends.

"I thought it was fucking evil," Calla says.

"What?"

"What?" Calla mocks her. "What?"

"That's ridiculous."

"I wouldn't expect a girl of thirteen—"

"*Fifteen.*"

"—to understand. But it is evil. The illusiveness of time gussied up in some stupid montage. Life slipping away from you. Real life is that hour in the line, not the hour in the theater."

This is not a serious worldview, Wren thinks. "Did he feel the same way?"

Calla says, "Who?"

"Your boyfriend."

She scoffs. "He wasn't a boyfriend. He wasn't a friend, or much of a boy, to tell the truth." Calla actually enjoys this. Against the odds, Roger and his child bride have produced someone worth talking to. If only Wren could be saved from all the St. Cloud bullshit, she might stay that way.

Wren teleports her avatar out of the hole. Nothing for her effort but some clay and a few scraps of tin. Her rickety house stands now on a precipitous drop. She is too proud to ask Calla how to cover it up.

"So you think *The Clock* distances you from life," Wren says, "but *The Neighborhood* doesn't?"

"It's a slog, a miserable slog, and that's how you know it's life. You buy, you trade, you suffer, you argue. You're *in* the world, not just *of* it."

"But it's a safe slog." Wren can't believe this, from the woman who says that writing does nothing. "The faux thrill of a roller coaster isn't the same as the fear of running for your life."

"Walk to the river. Good, now right-click on that fisherman." He is jaunty in a yellow slicker and bucket hat, greets Wren on her approach. At her click, the pickaxe swings—bursts through his chest. His eyes turn to horrible, cartoonish X's and he crumples into a pile of clothes and bones. Blinks twice. Vanishes.

"What the ever-living Hell!" Wren's anxiety has a pulse.

"Tell me that's the faux thrill of a roller coaster."

"It is." Wren cannot keep the uncertainty from her voice. "But—"

"Relax. He'll respawn."

"There's blood on the pickaxe." A pickaxe, a knife, a gun, a fire. The family legacy of killing and dying. And the senselessness of it—unreasoning, unfeeling. She wishes she could reach through the screen and touch the fisherman's hand. Prove to him she's sorry with the warmth of her own blood. "Someone just watched themself die."

There's a knock at the door.

"Come in," Wren says. Come see what I've done—the hurt.

"It's locked!" James's voice. Wren lets him in. "God, it smells like a Hard Rock Cafe in here." Calla offers him the lukewarm onion rings. "Which of you is playing *The Neighborhood* and why are you a haunted bucket doll?"

"Auntie Calla is showing me."

James nibbles an onion ring. "Isn't *The Neighborhood*—"

"—played by losers instead of having a real life?" Wren finishes. Calla just smiles.

"I was going to say, like, a decade old."

"Talk to that guy, Wren," says Calla. "He'll sell you a week pass for cave access."

"Are you going to have me kill him too?"

"Good God," James says, "what have I been missing?"

"Genuinely nothing." Calla wants this moment to pass, and the sun to rise, and the world to keep on turning. She wants to get back to some semblance of life. But which life: The one she left in New York, or the life of *The Neighborhood*, or some occluse third option? She picks a long flake of leather from the chair and wavers between love and spite.

"It's Paper Bag Plastic Bag all over again," James says.

Wren: "What's—"

Calla: "Literally why do you remember that?"

"I was traumatized! I talked about it in therapy."

"Will anyone—"

"It's a perfect analogy," Calla says, "in that no one was ever harmed."

"What are you guys talking about!"

A beat. Calla and James laugh at the same moment.

"God bless our family," James says, "so insular that our own niece can't track what the fuck we're on about."

"You tell her." Calla stands. "Up!" she says to Wren. "Your aunt needs to resume her research."

"But I was going to explore the caves!"

Reluctantly, Wren quits. She will find a way to apologize to that fisherman. She will make him a necklace of some rare and beautiful metal.

"Paper Bag Plastic Bag," James says through a mouthful of onion, "was a game of your mother's invention."

Calla says, "It was basically Truth or Dare." In the Spitehouse basement, her avatar tugs at the vault door. Perhaps if you simply try enough times . . .

"Yeah, except it was only dares. You had to do whatever Eddie said."

"Rake the yard, get a stone from the creek."

"She'd hold one of our toys hostage. Mine was usually Blue Bear. And Calla's . . . ?"

"Like I fucking remember."

"Calla had this cloth doll meant to empower women. She was a factory worker. Or an army nurse?"

"A gas station attendant."

"Anyway." James takes another onion ring. Nourishment to make it through this night. "You'd come back with the leaves raked. The snail you'd been told to find. Whatever. And if you'd done a good job, Edna would slip your toy in a paper bag—a lunch sack, a grocery bag. And she'd roll up the top and hold it there before your eyes. She'd describe the musty darkness inside. Blue Bear was in the dark, but nothing could hurt him. 'Bears like the dark,' she said. 'They spend a third of their life hibernating. Slumbering far from the real world.'"

It was like Blue Bear was really in a cave. Like if James wandered far enough, he might find his beloved toy's double—living, life-size. Those same paws he slept beside every night, suddenly enormous.

"Mine was called Pauline," Calla admits. "Eddie always pretended the bag was her apartment. She'd gone home after a long day of pumping gas. She heated up her TV dinner but couldn't bother to turn on the TV. There were sounds from the street. Trucks passing.

Kids' bikes with cards in the spokes. 'Pauline is safe. No one has a key to this door but her.' But the plastic bag . . ."

James says, "If you'd done a bad job—missed a spot with the leaves, say—she put the toy in a clear plastic bag. She sealed it up. And cubic milliliter by cubic milliliter, she'd squeeze all the air out."

Pauline's face was distorted by the vacuum. Squashed flat and broad. Calla's own breaths shallower in sympathy. It returned to her when she couldn't sleep. Someday, someone would tiptoe into her room and put a giant plastic bag around her. For a moment it would be beautiful—this membrane between the world and you. All the edges Plasticine-softened. Her life leaving, one thread of air at a time. And some strong hand would carry the bag from the house, and she'd bump against their body in time with their steps.

"'Now Pauline's having trouble thinking,' Eddie would say. 'She can feel a burning in her lungs. Her swimming head reminds her of a double shift. Gasoline fumes soaking her clothes until her breath is more gas than air.'"

James and Calla enjoy this. The proof they had not suffered alone. So much better to have a second archivist of these feverish traumas.

"'Blue Bear feels his limbs grow heavy. He's far from home and doesn't know how to get back.'"

"'Her earliest memories return to her. The girl who tackled her in the playground and cut off half her hair. The cake her grandmother made for her tenth birthday that her mother wouldn't let her eat.'"

"'His neurons firing. He thinks he feels freedom. The cool press of water.'"

"'And in the last moments of consciousness—'"

"'In the last gasp of his bear-y life—'"

"'She thinks, *This is what I deserve.*'"

"'He thinks, *This is the way of things.*' I had nightmares about it," James says. "Like, a lot of nightmares actually."

Calla can't say where those toys are now. For a second, it's important they be found. Maybe they're stored in plastic bags, suffocating. They probably are. How else do you store a toy? You'd want something impermeable to moisture and mold. To air. Their faces probably permanently disfigured. If Calla doesn't find Pauline—

"Totally stupid," she says.

"You guys are messing with me," Wren says. Her mother wouldn't so much as watch violent movies, no matter if everything turned out okay.

"Yeah, totally," James says. Soft, like a lung's last puff of air.

Another knock at the door. In pleasing unison, all say: "Come in!"

Heather's voice now: "It's locked!"

James opens the door. Eases it to and fro. Studies the frame, the hinges. "Did you lock this?" he asks Wren.

Heather on the threshold. "James, can—"

"Sorry, H.! Right this way." The munificent gesture of a carnival barker. "We have a murder cave and onion rings."

Heather doesn't enter. "Would you mind, actually, coming back to the room?"

Calla turns from her game. Is Heather going to break up with him? That would be perfect for tonight. They could get shit-faced. They could break all the rules and stumble into the streets and throw firecrackers down the storm drains. Sixteen, seventeen again.

James says, "Sure thing."

Wren leaps up from the gnarled chair. "I'll follow you guys out," she says. "I'm a hundred pages from the end of *The Brothers Karamazov*, and I might as well finish."

As they file out, Calla asks, "Would you guys leave the door open?" Her room has that plastic-bag feeling.

But they are already gone, and the door is shut.

ELEVEN

IT IS HARD to recall the shock of understanding. Thirty-six hours in and out of consciousness. It is hard for Edna to remember the strength it took to pull the knife from her shoulder. But it's easy to recall the hatred. Even if it kills me, she thought. At least if it kills me I will see Bea.

She goes on flipping through photos. Amazed she'd had the presence of mind to take them. All her life turns around that night. Thirty minutes that gave her Roger, and Wren, and her career. She was brave before—assertive, calculating, unflappable; she was brave after. But there is a part of her forever knife-pinned to that moment, seventeen and shaking with fear and rage. All her old life leaking from her in a steady, iron drip.

That part isn't in the photos. People want the fighter, the survivor—the girl with the knife in her hand, not the girl with it still in her chest.

Other things are missing. Waking from her uneasy sleep to find her father by the hospital bed. He was looking into space when her eyes cracked open. An enormous disappointment on his face. The injustice of it—that his life, his family, should be reduced to this. And then he noticed that she was awake, and the look of disappointment didn't vanish. *How could you not have known?* he asked her. The question repeated for weeks, years to come—by Bea and Polly's parents, by stricken girls at gas stations, by boys who thought she must have been in on the whole thing. *How could you not have known?* Twins were supposed to be close. To know what the other was thinking. She must be a killer herself. Her parents must be devil worshippers. A family of monsters, ready to snap at any moment.

How could she not have known? It would have become the question of her life if not for Roger. He was the only one who could piece together what happened. The garish X's slashed into her best friends. Her brother's fixation with women's bodies. The dolls. She and Roland had come into the world on the same day—had the same childhood, the same shot at happiness. She could not have been closer to him if she tried; but her twin had been put together wrong. It was Roger who helped her see, during those sleepwalking days of dry toast and hate mail, that she never could have known. That knowing would have done no good.

There was still the guilt, yes, and the unsteady beat of a broken heart. She should have been able to save them. She should have died herself. No photo, or book, or movie captures this—the flimsiness of everything. A light comes on and you see: the wall that's always protected you is only a scrim. You lean on it and it—breaks.

But Roger gave her the story. Gave her the ritual. Safety, and motion.

ROGER TYPES NOTES from his interview with Diana. He couldn't convince her to address the rumors: it was her mother's boyfriend, Ron, who'd done the killings; her mother had committed only two murders herself, copycatting some more prolific killer. He didn't need her approval to dive into these things. But you must be very careful how you betray your subjects. He's been sued for each book he published since *Doll Parts*.

If only he and Diana could spend some real time together without a ticking clock dragging him back to Virginia. There is a story here that needs telling. The role of the true-crime author in the twenty-first century is much like that of the fabulist in the nineteenth—id est, a cautionary illumination of the world's darkest corners. In many ways, he is a public servant. He ought to get a government pension. Copies of his books in every school library.

Look at Heather, after all. Worried about some sicko penetrating the house's battlements. The only way you could prevent these things from recurring was to study their every facet and edge. Perhaps you could lock up likely candidates before they committed their crimes. Send them to work an oil rig, far from ordinary society.

Roger laughs at the image—a bunch of fairies with crude black stains on the skirts of their pink tutus. He must remember to share this with Diana. He must see her soon.

He always knew he'd sleep with her. It never struck him as anything but a kind of research—knowing Diana, *hah*, inside and out. But the longer he interviewed her, the more time they spent in each other's company and in bed, the more she impressed him with her resilience. Her only concession to fear was a gun in her bedroom. Instead of sealing herself away, she went to classes and concerts and galleries and beaches. She wanted to control the narrative because she had a backbone. There was none of Edna's seventeen-year-old self, shaking with shock and hospital cold, in Diana.

He had to do—something. For the book, for his family. They would understand. If not right away, then later.

TWELVE

THE COPY OF *Doll Parts* is on James's bed. The TV is paused, but not where he left it. Edna with the knife in her shoulder. Pale and bloody fingers around its handle. If we did not know how this story went, we might think she was pushing it deeper.

"Been watching without me, eh?" James says.

Heather wishes that she had a fucking cigarette. "What do you mean?"

In one motion he grabs the remote, flops onto the bed, and unpauses the movie.

They can make a life together, she wants to say, but they don't have to. Or: they will always have each other, but there are so many forms having might take. She wants to put her hands on his chest, run her fingers through his hair, and fuck him until all words vanish from her mind. She says, "Can we not—"

"It's almost over."

"You know how it ends."

The girl on-screen pulls out the knife. The sound of a decades-old monster from the basement. He and Heather were once good at putting off life. In college they'd goad each other into staying up all night watching every Tarkovsky movie. They'd drag the other across campus to complete a scavenger hunt—polished stones hidden in the cracks of the sidewalk, a locket stamped with the date of their first kiss. Their finals, their fights, their sleep and sustenance—everything could wait.

Heather rips the DVD player's power cord from its socket.

James says, "Aww."

"James."

"Heather."

"Are we going to talk about the other night?"

Why frame it as a question unless she wants him to say no? Why force it? It's so embarrassing, being a person.

James flips through *Doll Parts*. "I see you've been diving into the sacred texts." He is almost mimicking girlhood, Heather thinks, sinking. His legs jackknife behind him as he reads. All he needs is a princess phone, a cord to wrap around his finger while he talks to the captain of the football team.

"*Everyone who saw them,*" James reads, "*remembered the dolls. By the time he was twelve, Roland St. Cloud was displaying his work at art fairs across Central Virginia and the Carolinas. There was a story about him in the local* News & Advance, *a photo of him at his workbench. A coterie of humanoid figures before him. He looks here like a mad God in a too-large sweatshirt, lording over His congregation of worshippers.*"

Heather crosses her arms. She's done begging.

"*Roland took commissions from lawyers and doctors and university professors—friends of his parents who wanted something unusual for a birthday, a christening gift. It was the faces, they said, that were special. It was the face, Roland said, that* is *the doll. A body can be anything: a bird's nest of yarn, a fistful of keys. As long as there's a face, life will follow.*"

"Are you done?"

"*It was around the time he turned thirteen that the dolls took a more sinister form. Where once he had sculpted high and rosy cheeks, a swish of coiffed walnut hair—now his work was all craggy hags, flesh pitted by his bent gouge. He was the demiurge and these, his martyrs.*"

"I know this is a bad time."

The book snaps shut. "No, Heather, it's the worst goddamn time you can imagine."

She loves him so much, is the thing. That is a reason to stop, and a reason to keep pushing.

"I think your brother-in-law is having an affair."

"Let the motherfucker," James says.

"You don't mean that."

"Who knows what I mean. What any of it means."

There is still a gulf between them. A step and a step and a step and she would be on top of him. The ache in her satisfied. They wouldn't need to say a word.

"You sound ridiculous," Heather says.

"I don't know if you've been paying attention but it's sort of the anniversary of when my monster brother carved up a bunch of girls."

"Which is not an excuse to avoid—"

"Avoid what, Heather? Why don't you tell me what you think happened."

She has always loved boys despite this tendency, this refusal to look difficulty in the face. From the first time she fucked her high school boyfriend on his parents' basement couch, she could not imagine a life without this. The beauty of his cock; his warm come on her hand. And if Jamie isn't—is—if James—

"Don't try to act like this is nothing," she says.

"Oh, it's something all right. I think anyone would agree with that."

"James."

"Your boyfriend asks you to dress him in your skirt. Fuck him in the ass. We invested—what, sixty, seventy bucks in the strap-on?"

She closes the distance now. Too late, maybe. "James," she says. "James. Jamie."

"You start to fuck him and neither of you is really into it but, what the Hell, you're already balls deep so—" On the bed she cups the back of Jamie's head and he pushes her away and she cups it again. His chestnut hair is baby-soft. "—you keep going and when you get in the groove of it, you see your boyfriend's dick is rock fucking solid. It may be the hardest you've ever seen it. Good golly, why doesn't he get it up like this for you normally?"

She had thought that. But: "You know that's not what I—"

Now he stands. Now he's putting distance between them, now closing it. Yo-yoing across the small bedroom. He doesn't look at Heather but at the dark reflection of them in the TV's dead eye.

"The skirt," he says, "the fucking tartan skirt flapping around his thighs. It's going to be ruined after this, you know, stretched and flabby and splattered with lube. And he's whispering something to you. And you lean close."

"Stop, James, stop."

He would be hard-pressed to account for a single thought he's had in the last ten minutes. There's only been this: the animal fear of something trapped.

"What's he whispering, Heather?"

"Stop."

"*EHHHH.*" Wrong answer. "Try again."

"This isn't what I wanted to happen."

"Well that makes goddamn two of us. What's he whispering?"

All the silence in the room has been used up. Heather clears her throat; she cannot stumble on this. "'Tell me I'm a good girl.'"

"And then he sobs like a homo. And you start crying too." Red-faced and exhausted, he sinks to the floor. Legs crossed. Eyes level with Heather's body and the rumpled moonscape of his childhood bed. He shouldn't have brought her here. Not with this hanging over them.

"Jamie," Heather says. "Are you—"

"Don't you fucking dare ask me that. Not tonight, not ever."

"But *are* you?"

"No, Heather. For fuck's sake."

"So, what, then?" Relief. This has been reduced to a linguistic problem. Heather bites her lip the way she once did during chem problem sets. They'd go home from the library together, and after hours of concentration, there'd be a staple-shaped dent in the lip's center. Jamie would kiss it until the impression faded. "You're—bi? Gay?"

"It's not—" James says. A hospital-waiting-room silence. Good news will come, or bad. If you're the praying type, this might be the time to offer something up. If not to God, then to the universe, the sterile walls, the crime show reruns.

"It's hot for you, right?" Heather says. "It's hot for me. I mean, besides the crying."

"What?"

How oddly salvation comes. Not needing words, not needing definition. They bumped against his self-ignorance, his inability to define what he wants, and they had rolled right past it. Because he has no idea what he is. No idea what he wants. The words (*Tell me I'm—*) had not entered his head until the moment he said them. When she'd been inside him, it was the only language left to him.

Heather is grinning now. Adjusting herself to mirror his position. There she is, legs crossed on the bed above him. His sage, his savior.

"Of course I found it hot, babe. I wouldn't have agreed to it otherwise." It isn't as lovely as having him inside her. But she enjoys the power. Watching his cock bounce in time with her thrusts, hearing his little throaty moans. Heather is wet just thinking about it.

"It's so hot for me," he admits. "Yeah. Like a fetish." He's never had a fetish before. His porn searches hopelessly ordinary. He might not recognize . . .

"Come up here."

He stands, wobbles. Tackles Heather onto the bed. Both laughing.

"I love you."

"I love you so much, J." She kisses him hard. Presses against him until they roll over and he is under her. "I should have brought the—the strap."

"Yeah?"

"We have all this night to kill."

From the far side of the bed, Roger's book mocks him. He chucks it across the room, pulls Heather closer. Their bodies entwined like old ivy.

"You didn't have to come here, H., and I'm never going to forget that you did."

"Oh, Jamie."

"I mean it. We're going to drive home tomorrow and we're going to listen to every album from Peter Gabriel–era Genesis. We're going to keep sneaking out of work to share snacks and cigs and we're going to throw a party for all our friends." Heather usually has to drag James from the house by his heels; she is too pleased to question this. "I'm going to shake down Edna for three hundred dollars," he goes on, "and I'm going to spend every one of them on a preposterous bouquet of flowers. It will be the sort of bouquet a poet could spend a hundred and thirty lines naming."

"I don't need any of that, James."

"You deserve every flower, every stanza, because you love me."

They kiss. Longer, now.

And when they part: "Do you mind if we finish the movie?"

Heather cannot but laugh—short, breathy. She will laugh like this a lot over the next year. "This family and your rituals."

"They keep us sane." He plugs in the DVD player, waits for the disc to spin to life. "So, Roger's cheating on Eddie?"

THIRTEEN

THE KITCHEN. EDNA at the table, still, with her catalog of photos. She flips by an essay written for the exhibit. She does not need to see the word *wunderkind* ever again.

Tomorrow there will be regular problems. Groceries to buy, coffee to make, coursework for Wren. The gallery. Most nights she waits an hour to fall asleep, thinking, I can't believe I have to lie here like this every night of my life.

She makes herself love it. The life this ritual allows. Eating at this table while Wren shares some fact she learned about the Peloponnesian War. These are the things we trade: her friends died and so she has her family, this house—this one safe place; these walls protected by light and blood. Her parents—

It's worth it, is the thing. She feels horrible thinking it but it's true. For this life, this very life.

Roger comes in. "Ah! Here you are!" Swoops in, kisses her. She kisses back and her eyes return to the book. "I've been all over the house," he says. "Windows locked up tight. Nothing in the corners. Smooth sailing until morning's landfall."

"And the burglar alarm?"

"Armed and ready and paid through the next year. We'll be alerted to any crack in our armor."

"Thank you, dear."

The book lies open to the first photo she took after coming home. She'd had her week in the hospital, a month in a hotel to decompress. No one but her parents came in or out. And then back to this place, with all its open windows and doors. The photo bears an expression she still catches in the mirror now. The shock of survival. Still a child and never a child again.

Roger says, "Is there—nothing else I can do?"

It's worth it, it's all worth it.

A sob ricochets through her.

"Edna!" Roger crouches beside her, hands bracketing her shoulders. "Edna, dear doe. What can I do?"

It's almost like hiccuping—this arrhythmic, convulsive crying.

"It's," she says, "all so stupid."

"It's a fragile time of year."

"I know that."

"You can feel the day coming, fear and time hand in hand—"

"Roger, shut up for one second and let me cry."

Roger does not think of his book, or Diana Cutter, or the night nineteen years past that he immortalized. For this moment he thinks only of Edna. He keeps crouching as his knees stiffen, lock. Afraid that if he lifts his hand from her shoulder, she will burst again. Candlelit, reflected in the window against the screen of night, they might still be children. Their wrinkles blurred and gray hairs indistinct. No time might have passed, Roger thinks, since that decisive night. Their first meeting one endless day. He would do it all again; he would stumble through those nineteen years to be here, with Edna—with her red face and snot and tears.

"Do you want to talk about it?" he says.

"It's the same things as always."

"If I didn't believe that repeating stories mattered, I wouldn't have a career."

It's the revenge of the for-wants: for want of seeing evil coming; for want of going to college. For want of living parents. If she'd moved to New York and no one ever knew her name. If she didn't need to be the linchpin for her fucked-up siblings. For want of want of want of want—

"Was I ever more than a victim, Rodge?"

"Of course you were. You were the girl who fought back."

"What good is that? What does it mean except that I took the knife out of my chest and put it in someone else's?"

"If that's guilt I'm hearing—"

"Not guilt. Not anything." Still crying, but without sobs. The sort people mistakenly call brave-faced. The refrigerator hums and both of them jump; only Roger laughs. This is a room of peace. How many times had Edna described her parents cooking dinner with their arms around each other? Never mind that a monster grew up eating at this same Formica table; there is a burning candle to keep him away. No bad thing will cross this threshold.

"You're getting tears on the book," he notices.

"Let it rot."

"It's a collectible."

She used to find charming his thrift, his money-conscience. The delight Roger took in soft cheeses and pâté. When she sits up, her tears fall only on herself.

"You know what I see when I look at these photos?" Edna says. "I see shit composition, the wrong exposure, lighting without drama. The only thing I can see to care about is me. Poor, tortured little girl."

"It's natural as our art progresses that we think less of old work."

"Is that how you feel about my story, now?"

"You know that isn't what I meant," he says.

"Well, it isn't what I meant either. Was there ever anything there, Rodge? Was it art at all, or did people only want a piece of my fetid fucking soul?"

"You're being dramatic, Ed."

She throws the book from the table. "Tell me there was, then! Tell me I'm fucking wrong!"

Roger retrieves the book, performs brushing it off. There's not a hair, not a pinprick of dirt on the spotless linoleum. The St. Cloud parents raised all these kids the same.

"You know what I see when I look at these pictures?" he asks. "I see the way you laughed when I first met you. Laughed right in my face."

"Probably so I wouldn't cry."

"At the coffee shop. You laughed. Your parents hesitated but I showed them I was harmless. It was the first time you left the house."

The problem wasn't leaving, but avoiding the wrong parts of the house. She'd press her ear to the wash of wall where her brother's door had been, listening to her blood's white noise until she felt sick. The Geiger counter in her heart ticked when she approached the downstairs bathroom, the entryway, the basement—they'd leave her DNA full of holes, her fingernails falling out, her dreams full of twisted hallways and hands grasping from the walls. She returned to these places, hurting herself until it hurt too much.

"I told you I didn't have an agenda," Roger says, "that all I wanted was the truth."

"And that made me laugh."

"So defiant. So brilliant and sharp and alive. Now as you ever were."

"I told you, 'The truth is that all my friends are dead.'"

"You did what they couldn't. You saved yourself."

"No," Edna says. "Bea saved me." She hesitates. "You know I thought I saw her the other day?" Edna's tears have dried up. "She was coming down the aisle of the grocery store. A basket filled—almost past the point of carrying it—with canned peaches. A tiny aerosol can of whipped cream. She looked exactly like Bea. And I realized the girl was probably a college student, out on her own for the first time, spending her student loan money on too much sweetness to celebrate the end of her freshman year. She'd probably go back to a dormitory, to cheap wine and Never Have I Ever. She'd probably fuck her boyfriend on some rickety bottom bunk. Her stomach full of peaches, and syrup, and the tiniest bit of cream. I wanted to follow her, wherever she went. I wanted to take a picture—not for a show, but for me."

Edna breaks gently as she says: "I realized that girl was probably born after. That she and Bea never shared the Earth."

"You should have told her. She would have been touched."

"Hah. She would have thought I was a criminal."

"She might have let you take a picture."

"And then I'd have to bring it home and develop it. And as that ghostly face came rising up through the developer, I'd have to confront the fact that it didn't really look like her. That all I had was a picture of a stranger. No, it's better this way. With only the memory."

"You'd get a good story out of it, anyway."

"I'm tired of being a good story," Edna says. "I worry that's all I've ever been: a cocktail fact to trot out when the party runs out of wine."

"Edna—"

"I'm a good photographer, right? A good mother?"

"You're the best." He closes her hands around the catalog, kisses her fingers. "My favorite photographer. My favorite mother."

"I worry about Wren."

Out of the woods now, Roger gives her his biggest smile. He can't imagine Diana breaking down this way. Soon there will be the Pacific beaches' warm sand and icy water. A certain polka-dot swimsuit . . .

"No one escapes childhood without a little trauma," he says.

"I worry she's lonely." A beat. "What do *you* mean?"

"Only—what I say. Growing up, fighting for a place in the world. As with that business in the middle school. It leaves a mark on us, even those who do not fight as you fought."

"When's the last time she saw any of her friends—Joan, or Freddie, or Clark?"

"They go for walks, sometimes. Sleepovers."

"When? What's the last story you remember her telling about them?" Roger has nothing. "He didn't have friends either," Edna says.

"It isn't the same."

"It doesn't have to be the same. It would be enough for it to be very, very similar."

"It isn't," says Roger.

"How can you know? How can you know that, any more than I can? It's worse now, with the internet. The kinds of stories you can find."

"You're spiraling, Ed."

"That's right. Right down the drain."

Into her eyes go the heels of her hands. The darkness sparkling. It's only when she hears Roger unlock the window that she sits up straight. Surely he isn't—but there is the gentle knife of spring wind. There is the alarm. Roger slams the window shut.

"What the *fuck* were you thinking?" she demands.

"Some fresh air—"

"Oh sure. Some *fresh air*." Edna stands, throws the window back open. The alarm does not stop; Roger will have to put in the code. Soon everyone in the house will come to check, to see what monsters have breached the ritual's shield. They will see her face, puffy and red. And Roger, useless against life's furies. "Why not stab me in the chest, Rodge?"

"You're being—" Ridiculous. Unwifely. A harridan. "You're safe, Edna." He closes the window, crosses to the keypad, silences the alarm. Edna collapses again into her chair.

"Sometimes I wonder if my parents intended us to live here," she says. "Or if they left it to us so we could tear it down."

FOURTEEN

THE BASEMENT, LIT by camping lantern. Wren sits on two stacked milk crates in the corner, craning over her copy of *The Brothers Karamazov*. The basement is long since cleared of Roland's tools and dolls. Only his old workbench remains, buried beneath countless boxes of St. Cloud family detritus. Marked-up playscripts, dusty trophies, cheap china. The Grampus's food and water bowls. Still, when Wren hides down here to read, she sometimes finds the odd bit or bob: a varnished splinter, a spool of thread, a piece of cloth cut into the tiny outline of a hand.

Roger heaves down the stairs. Wren closes the book, waits.

"Dad?"

"Hello, Wrennie!"

He finishes his descent. The strings that hold Wren slacken.

"You always know by the sound of our steps," Roger says.

"I learned from Mom. Sitting in the kitchen while you or Grandpa or Grandma came up the walk. Who, and how many, and who would reach the door first."

"The alarm didn't bother you?"

"It never goes off except by mistake."

"Such a learned little one." He quotes: "*I go on living in spite of logic. Though I may not believe in the order of the universe, yet I love the sticky little leaves as they open in spring*. How are the Brothers treating you?"

"Good, only—they won't really let Dmitri be sent to Siberia, will they?"

"Even if he's guilty?"

"But he isn't. He can't be."

"Well. The only way to know is to read on."

Wren doesn't miss school one bit. The punch of disinfectant, the cacophony of locker doors, shoes squeaking in the halls. All the stupid facts she was expected to regurgitate. Everything she needs to learn can be learned in this house.

The surprising thing is that anyone wants more than a life of reading. What could she live that would compare with the glow of Ahab's harpoon? The taut moments of love unspoken between Ladislaw and Dorothea Brooke? She'd teased Calla about playing *The Neighborhood*, but here are her true feelings: the best parts of the world can be bought for roughly twelve dollars, with a black spine and the Penguin colophon.

Her dad lingers, weighing words.

"Is everything okay?" Wren asks.

"Oh yes, merely checking up. I thought you might be down here. Curled up in quiet study of the universe."

"I suppose it's a bit grim, isn't it? Being down here tonight?"

"Only if you feel you must carry your mother's wounds."

"The basement doesn't just belong to her, though. There's all the stuff Grandma and Grandpa left behind. And their parents' stuff, and their parents' parents.' "

Roger would be the person to ask about St. Cloud Petrochem, Wren knows. The fire. Flesh burning like chicken thighs abandoned on the grill. He would give an honest answer.

"Not everyone is so lucky," he says, "as to inherit their family's history."

Roger's childhood was haunted by divorce, banks, and bankruptcy. From one rented room to another. A trailer washed away in hurricane floods.

"One day," Wren says, "I'll go through every box. I'll catalog every piece and choose what stays and what goes. Most of it will go."

"Your children, should you have them, may not thank you for that."

"My children, should I have them, would be grateful for the space. I'll pin string lights over the bowers. A rug, a lamp, an electric kettle for tea."

"It won't be much of a place to hide," Roger says, "if you make it hospitable as that."

"Why would they need a place to hide?"

"Oh, Wrennie. My little bird." Perhaps Edna is right. It isn't natural for a girl of fifteen to be so close to her parents. What if she becomes some spinster aunt, haunting this old house past his death, past Edna's? She'll have read every book worth reading by the time she's forty; what will she do with the latter part of her life?

The voice niggling at his hindbrain: *One more reason to go. Show her it can be done.*

"I wish you wouldn't linger down here," he says. He didn't come down intending to be honest. "It isn't good for any of us."

"Not now, Dad. Not tonight."

"Tonight most of all, love. Surely you can see—"

"I'm not afraid of this place, Dad. Everyone else is. Even you. Everyone except for Mom."

What could she possibly mean? Oh, the misguided certainty of youth!

"Be that as it may—"

"I mean it," Wren says, "whose choice was it to live here?"

"There were lots of factors at play, as you likely remember, including—"

"It was Mom's."

"I suppose, if we must pin it on someone . . ."

"Do you not remember what it was like in our old house? Every unfamiliar corner, every slightly too-dark shadow? Do you remember how she used to stare into the laundry chute, waiting for something to rise up and harm her?"

A pause.

"Yes."

"People act like Mom is crazy for coming back here. People say the floors are soaked with blood. But isn't that how they protected buildings in the old days? Put a corpse in the walls?"

"If certain legends are to be believed, yes."

"This is the place she knows best. Why go somewhere else? You can die anywhere."

Yes, he must leave. Not forever, not for long. Only a taste of freedom. An object lesson in the beauty of the faraway. He will not die in this house. His daughter will not.

"You remember Kolya Krasotkin?" Wren says. "The boy who lies under moving trains to prove how brave he is?"

"He passes out from fear, as I recall."

"That's what protects him. He can't move when he's unconscious."

And that's exactly what we cannot be like, Roger does not say. He is filled with a heat, a longing, a love so limitless it cannot care about hurting. He needs Wren to understand.

"Wrennie, you know that I love you so much."

"I love you, too, Dad." A beat. "What's this about?"

"Only the tenor of the night. In my wildest dreams, never did I imagine I'd be standing in this basement with my teenage daughter, talking about Dostoevsky."

"That isn't all, though."

One of his knees, still stiff from crouching beside Edna, buckles. "I assure you it is."

"No, tell me. Whatever I can imagine is worse than the truth."

"There's nothing else, Wren. What else could there possibly be, on a night like tonight?"

FIFTEEN

IT WASN'T FROM her parents that Calla got the idea to be a playwright—it was from Iris Murdoch. She read *The Sea, The Sea* during an unusually stormy summer, curled in the windowless room that's now Edna's darkroom. There was a couch and a lamp and nothing else; all the Heavens' sounds diminished by the walls within walls. She was fifteen, then, and would remain afraid of thunderstorms until her parents died.

But *The Sea, The Sea*. Its loathsome Charles Arrowby, retired director and playwright, with his disgusting meals of boiled onion. You can't help being captivated by him. *The theater is an attack on mankind carried on by magic*, he says. *To victimize an audience every night, to make them laugh and cry and suffer and miss their trains.* And further: *Drama must create a factitious spell-binding present moment and imprison the spectator in it.* She'd been determined to cast that spell, to make the audience her victims. To seed their hearts with every base and blessed condition. She wanted to write worlds so intense that the actors could not leave them behind. They'd go home at night to their boyfriends and wives with those lines on their tongues, those gestures in their bones.

This is why she's never respected Edna's photography. It offers only static glimpses of a pathetic little world: her portraits, family photos; the shots of the house and the tokens of so many St. Cloud generations. It is small. You can walk right past it untouched.

Calla's first play, *Lethargy*, had a sold-out off-Broadway run before her twenty-third birthday. Her second, *Dynamo*, repeated that feat before moving to Broadway. It was with *Shield* that she tried to do something else, to shake off her husband-wife and best-friend dyads and write about a family. Not her family, mind; just *a* family. The complicated betrayals and grudges and secret lives. Audiences fucking ate it up. But they left the theater amiably chatting. They were not devastated, not transformed; no one missed their trains. They left her perfect, ugly world behind for a cup of decaf, a slice of cake. For, *Should we plant gardenias this year?* For, *How's your sister's baby?* Stupid, ordinary. They thought they were safe once that curtain fell. Free from the ugliness and discomfort.

Real art was like that guy who spent a year punching a time card every hour. Who spent a different year tied to another artist with an eight-foot rope. Real art was grueling and consuming and not done by anyone with a right mind or clean conscience.

People filter through the Spitehouse. Calla put out a call for assistance and this is who answered: curled blonde hair, a ten-gallon hat, a human body with an octopus head. Messages fill the empty halls and rooms as they explore.

Nice place here, the people say. *Could use some furniture though.* Calla can't be bothered to refurnish each time she burns the place down. *How'd you design that frame?* She could kill these awkward gawkers. *Violence is born of the desire to escape oneself*—another Murdoch book. *What redeems us is that speech is divine.*

Calla writes: *Come look in the basement. That's where it is. That's where I need help.*

Easy to ask for, here in the game. She isn't Calla St. Cloud or a person at all. She's a distorted body, a living Giacometti sculpture named RIP_OFF_RED.

This is why *The Neighborhood*. This is why she gave up writing. You go into this world and you become it. You reshape it. It becomes your life and stays that way. It is real, absolutely real.

They line up before the vault, these would-be Excalibur-pullers, confident they will find the trick. Calla has offered to split whatever is in there fifty-fifty.

These are tools from the wizard in the Hollowing Woods, someone named sawdustanddiamonds619 says. *Supposedly they can open any door.*

"All right, all right," Calla says. "Don't make this more embarrassing than it already is." She winces as the supposed magic lockpick shatters against the vault door. This is real. People get married and die in *The Neighborhood*. They make monuments to their hubris and find ladders to the moon and spend hours in café-bars talking about art until their screens go fuzzy with simulated drunkenness.

Someone named MiekeShaw is next to approach. A blonde girl in an A-line dress. *I heard about this puzzle in a hedge maze*, she says. *It had something to do with the real-life moon phases and the moon phases in-game*. She turns the vault's wheel all of about three degrees before it stops. *You should start recording how far this turns each day. I bet you anything it's not consistent.*

Off to the side stands a humanoid figure—skin pitch-black and dotted with stars. *Look at your f—ing house, Red*, they say. Their name is BegottenBegottenBegotten. *Look at your little Laura Ingalls fantasy. RPing suburbanity in the year of our lord Two Thousand Elevene. Why don't you growu p. Why don't you play the game like an adult.*

Okay, Calla types. *So am I to understand that no one has seen anything like this firsthand?*

Sure we've seen something like it, someone else writes. *It's a door. It'll open when it's time to open. Where the Hell did it come from, though?*

Before Calla can equip a sword and kill this guy, MiekeShaw intervenes. *If you read Red's call, you'd know it appeared after they burned the house down like a hundred times.*

Begotten says: *Red I am going to find you and you are going to be married and have a dog and a picket fense and I am going to burn down your house for you. I am going to watch the flames dance through the windows and I am going to save your fdog and train him to hate. I am going to train him to hurt. I am going to bring him to your hospital bed, where you will be barely breathing and grafted in new skin and I am going to have him eat it all off like it is so much crispy chicken.*

Someone named Herland private messages Calla: *Jesus Cuh-RIST what is that guy's problem.*

Idk, Calla writes. *People are so deranged in here. Like—I'm pretty obviously NOT role-playing perfect suburban life??? Literally I keep burning down my house??*

Herland: *It's like very obviously a violent strain of misogyny. Probably a repressed fag if we're being honest.*

Calla cackles. *Yeah what do you need all that void for, Begotten? Some guy's big meaty COCK?*

Herland: *EW pls do not say c*ck.*

Herland: *I know this house btw.*

Herland: *This is the St. Cloud house.*

Oh god, Calla writes, *are you some kind of true-crime nut?*

Herland: *You're one to talk.*

Herland: *My friends and I used to ring the doorbell when we were kids. Hoping we'd catch sight of a ghost or something.*

Herland: *What's YOUR excuse?*

Edna knocks; Calla is in the Spitehouse, Calla is in the fucking former playroom. There is the vault on the screen and the twin bed, the window, the bare walls all around her. Her sister tests the knob, enters.

"You should lock that, Calla," Edna says.

"You're telling me."

My excuse? Calla types. *I literally live in that house.*

Edna asks, "You weren't bothered by the alarm?"

"Didn't hear it." Edna fusses with the still-made bed. Flattening out the folds, patting the pillows. She scrutinizes the plate of onion ring crumbs next to Calla. "You should've sent your little househusband to do that too," Calla says.

"What?"

"He came by before. Made sure to tell me how *happy* you are to have me here."

"I am happy to have you here," Edna says.

"Oh yeah, you're so happy. That's why it's taken you half the night to come see me."

"Why else would I be up here?"

To do what Mom used to do, Calla thinks. To make sure I still keep my bed hospital-cornered. To see that my suitcase is neatly stowed in the closet and there aren't clothes all over the floor. Because who cares how your life *is* so long as it *looks* tidy. "You like having me home because it proves things aren't as fucked-up as they could be," she says. "You can keep an eye on me like you do Jamie. See how deep the damage goes."

Edna laughs, takes the plate to the bathroom next door and rinses it free of crumbs. She goes on laughing. A burbling stream of it beneath the running water.

"What?" Calla says.

Edna takes her time with the plate. Shakes it clean of drops, dries it with a square of tissue. What was merely funny is becoming hysterical. She returns in a storm of laughter.

"Stop it." Calla will not be mocked. She has punched men for less—socked them square in the chin. Edna laughs harder still. "What! Goddammit, Eddie." Calla stands, shakes her sister by the shoulders. "What's so goddamn funny!"

Edna reins it in. Deep breaths, cheeks aching. "You think—you think I care how damaged you are?"

"You fucking well ought to."

Another laugh, her spit flecking Calla's face. It has been seven years since Calla cried, but she feels that ancient eye-ache now. She shoves her sister away, returns to her laptop.

"I'm sorry, I don't mean it personally, Calla." Nothing from Calla. She is burning down the Spitehouse again. All those gawkers still inside. She is breaking pickaxe after pickaxe against the unyielding vault door. "Calla. Calla. Calloh-callay. Callalily."

"Don't call me that."

"I only—"

"You aren't Mom."

People stream from the burning building. Calla's avatar is crushed beneath the wreckage, blinks back to life seconds later beside the blighted lot. And then Herland messages: *Which one are you?*

Which one do you want me to be?

"I'm sorry," Edna says. "I only mean it's too late for all of us. You know that, don't you, Callalily?"

They're all so goddamn sorry all the goddamn time. Why do they think sorrying does any good? Calla says, "Stop it."

"That's why you came home, isn't it? That's why you can't write."

"You have no idea what I can do."

Edna regards her sister. Still young, still beautiful. As Edna is herself. As Edna has not felt in nineteen years.

"You know, I was so excited when you were born. I decided it was going to be like those chapter books Mom used to read to us. Older sister and younger sister venturing into the woods or beneath the waves. We'd find a den of good-hearted thieves or a race of fishpeople who'd lost a holy relic."

"I wasn't your doll."

Edna flinches. "No. But I thought I might finally have a sibling who was—normal."

"You had a funny fucking way of showing it."

"What do you want me to say, Calla? I'm sorry about who I was when I was fifteen, sixteen? I don't know if you've noticed but we're all older now. I have a daughter."

"And I'm sure that fixed you." That and the murders. A heavy silence. Herland is typing.

"I always sort of liked that you didn't come home," Edna says. "Even when it made me sad. I thought it might mean you'd escaped."

I wish you were that murdering tranny, Herland writes. *So I could be the one to slit your throat.*

Where are you? Calla wants to see her avatar. Some sign, some figuration.

I'm looking through your windows, Herland writes. *Waiting for you to let me in.*

"Not my home," Calla says.

"I'm sorry?"

"It's your home. Not mine. Mom and Dad made absolutely sure of that."

"What do you want me to do about that?" Edna asks.

"I don't know, Eddie, what do you want us to do about Roland killing—"

"Don't say his name and do *not* compare those two things."

I'll leave a window cracked for you, she writes, and logs out. Calla will not be the one who waits. Edna tugs the sheets off the bed and remakes it.

"I need a home, Calla. Need one. I have a family—one I actually love—and my habits, my ways of being in the world. And you have your life in New York. Your life without us."

"It should've been ours," Calla says. "All of ours."

"James doesn't feel that way."

"You don't know what Jamie thinks. You think he wouldn't take the money?"

Calla used to know a hundred tricks to stave off crying. You fake a yawn and pretend your eyes are watering. You tip your head back so gravity pushes them down. But she is out of practice, and the more she thinks about crying the more she feels she's going to.

"I'd trade the money, the house, all of it, for someone else to have found them," Edna says. "Do you remember that, Calla? Do you think about the fact that I was here, with my daughter, not half a day after our parents died?"

Steady, now: "I don't think about you much at all, Eddie."

"I know you don't. You don't think about what it's like to step into our parents' warm vomit. How it might feel to have their last dregs of life stain the soles of your shoes. And you want to shout to keep your eight-year-old daughter from the room, and you know that shouting will only bring her. And though you can see the pill bottle in Mom's hand, there's a part of you that doesn't believe she could have done it. That somehow, *he* got in here, *he* did it to punish you. That you have always, only deserved punishment—because what just universe, what loving God, would allow this otherwise? One more tragedy you didn't see coming. And caught there, pinned to the moment like a butterfly no one bothered to etherize, you do the only thing you can think of. You get a bucket of soapy water. You bend down, not noticing how your knees get stained too. You'll be told later that you tainted a crime scene—but how could it be a crime, when there's no one left to punish? And you clean up your parents'—*our* parents'—dead bodies."

It would have implicated the kids if they'd known what their parents planned. The St. Cloud family dragged to the courthouse one more time. The logic of the suicide is perfectly clear, but this can't be the only reason for their parents' silence.

Seven years of silent tears slug down Calla's face. Edna does not notice.

"What would you do with this house if you had it, Callalily?"

"It doesn't matter." Her voice is even. Her years in the theater good for something. If Edna noticed, it would break the tension. There would be a moment of closeness that Calla could not stand.

"You'd sell it," Edna says. "You'd let someone else walk those floors I scrubbed. You'd have the basement and attic and all the rooms hold strangers' lives. And every day, we'd lose a little bit of ourselves."

"What do you think holding on has gotten you, Ed? A daughter too scared to step into the world? A floundering photography career? A husband who's cheating on you? People in witness protection have it best. They get a new place, a new name, a new script to follow. Nineteen years ago, you could have become anyone. You could've changed your name when you got married. Could have married anyone—a mobster, say, or the town drunk—instead of that fucking vulture. We could have parted as strangers, so that when we met some day on the plains of Purgatory, we might have met as allies." She sniffs once, wipes her nose on her hand. All her tears already dry. "Instead, here we are."

"It's enough that we're alive, Calla. That we're here and we're safe. And whatever I would trade the money for, I'd rather find Mom and Dad a thousand times over, their corpses forever fresh like the bodies of saints, than give up an inch of that safety."

"Did you hear me? I said Roger's sleeping with someone." Heather and James hadn't been able to keep their voices down.

"It doesn't matter," Edna says. Sad little Calla only knows how to punch.

"God, you're damaged."

"And so what? There's a lot of evil in the world. Someone has to take more than their share."

"You think that's why Mom did it?"

"It's as good a reason as any. Some people reach a point, they've taken all they can. But I'm miles out from there. I'm gripping the Earth with all my fingernails."

Isn't that why they all kept the red-yellow mark of this name? Proof they were venomous, might strike at anyone who passed in the high grass. Calla hadn't understood that till she tried writing under a pseudonym and found she had nothing to say.

"You know I went to see him yesterday?" Edna does not need to say who. "I go see him every year the day before. Not the anniversary of the killings, but the last day we were only—siblings. Twins. Not madman and victim. Not hunter and prey. Not that horrible faggot clown and—whatever I was. It helps me see him as a person. For a little while."

"I wasn't aware you ever thought of him as a person," Calla says.

"In the hospital he looks small and sad. He still can't make eye contact. He's a roll of unexposed film. The problem is that, in the two hours between hospital and home, I lose the feeling. I see that slackness as calculation. The reflected fluorescence is a spark in his eye. He's the horror movie villain we all turned him into. No depth past the rouge on his cheeks. By the time I'm almost home, I'm stopping at gas stations to make sure he isn't in the back seat."

Calla says, "You know what the solution is?"

"What?"

"Move him in here. Keep him close by so you can always see how empty he is."

Gelid terror slices through Edna, but laughter fights and wins. A few sharp barks. "God, that would be something to see. Chain him up in the basement, spit in his face before breakfast each morning."

"Not a jury in the world would convict you."

SIXTEEN

ON THE TV, the second *Dollmaker* movie plays. Heather is sleeping beside James. Through the window, the faintest hint of dawn.

"Heather. Hey, Heather."

"Hnnn?"

"Look." She turns her face across her shoulder. Sees the window but doesn't understand. "The night's ending," James says.

IN THE KITCHEN, Wren watches the burning candle. She's still wearing her mother's overalls. She can't decide if the flame is a good symbol for a human life. It would be so easy to mistime the burning, even after so many rituals. So easy to breathe a little too hard and—*poof*—turn light to air and smoke. Easy, too, for the fire to spread. To hurt.

Her mother enters—looking tired and happy. They're all manic with sleeplessness.

"Nearly morning," Edna says.

"It's always nearly morning somewhere, isn't it?" Wren says. "You could keep dividing back time, finding ways to prove to yourself it's a hundred days in the future or past."

"The body doesn't care. The body knows what day it is."

Roger enters, fiddling with his pen.

"This thrice-damned thing has been leaking all over my notes."

"Your unwritten words," Wren says, "blotting out the written ones. They're jealous."

Roger laughs. "Yes, I suppose. As the unconscious must envy the conscious. As day succeeds night and life succeeds sleep."

"Still alive," Edna says. "Still alive."

JAMES LEAVES HEATHER sleeping, toes across the landing to Calla's room. The door unlocked.

"Hello, Cal."

"Jamie."

"Morning out there."

"I'd noticed."

"Come on down to the kitchen."

"I don't—"

"I know you want to pretend it doesn't mean anything," James says, "but you didn't sleep last night either." Calla is typing messages to Herland. The game, the vault, the house. James doesn't relent. "There's no profit in lying. I know you as well as you know me."

"Your brain's been rotted by those horror movies, Jamie. You think everyone is full of double crosses and hidden agendas. The drowned boy's mother turns out to be the killer the whole time."

"Yeah, this isn't going to work on me." He holds out his hand. "Are you coming or aren't you?"

"I'm not."

"Wrong answer."

"I'm not!"

"All right, then."

He leaves the room, returns with a lumpy black trash bag. He holds it with both hands like the corpse of a beloved pet.

Calla says, "What the fuck is that?"

"It's your doll. The gas station attendant. I found her in Wren's room."

"Pauline?"

"She's still got a little air in there." The bag hisses as he presses. "But already her lungs are starting to ache."

"This isn't funny, James."

"She's had a long day at the gas station. Sometimes she works the counter inside. Selling gum to young mothers to mollify their screaming toddlers. Condoms to truckers and sheepish teenagers. When Pauline got home, she didn't bother to turn on the light. Only sat down in her kitchen chair."

"James, I swear to god—"

"When the fateful hand of God wrapped round her throat and breathless darkness descended—"

Calla rushes him, tears the bag from his hands. She rips away the plastic to reveal: only a throw pillow.

"I had you going," James says.

"You asshole."

He picks her up by the waist.

"Let go!" Calla thrashes but fails to break free.

"Weak-ass New York girl."

"You're such a bitch! You're such a little bitch!"

But she's laughing. James is laughing. Everyone is alive.

THE ST. CLOUD–MERRILOWS stand around the kitchen table. The sky lightens steadily. Soon they will be normal, or close enough. They will go back to being names whispered in slumber-party bedrooms, by historians of loss, by doorbell-ditch children and horror connoisseurs. They will have their year of days before returning to this Walpurgisnacht remembrance.

James carries Calla, still flailing, over the kitchen threshold and drops her on the linoleum floor.

"Asshole," Calla says.

James salutes. "St. Cloud family, present and accounted for. Also Roger."

"Not fair!" Wren says. "I'm not a St. Cloud."

Calla holds out a hand until her niece helps her up. "Yeah, you are."

"Oh, don't put that on her, Cal."

"She hasn't slept any more than we have."

"It's a miracle, isn't it?" Edna beams at the family collected. "Not that we survived this night, but that we survive any night. That any person goes on long enough to live a full life. That humans ever evolved the tools to keep out the wolves, the viruses, the men with knives. That we have houses, and light, and each other."

"Sure," Calla says. "Let's get it over with"

Wren plucks the candle from its stick. Out they traipse, a family line. They squint against the new day's light, stumble where their muscles have grown stiff. They march through the grass and the morning wind, the quiet breath that will always sound like childhood, like home. Wren leads them to the circle of stones in the backyard, and Roger pulls back the dewy blue tarp. Beneath is a cone of kindling and logs.

How would her mom react if the candle went out now? Would they have a year of terror, or would it free her?

But her father is already arranging balls of newspaper, already spraying lighter fluid across the wood. He isn't thinking about what comes next, only preparing the pyre. The candle keeps its flame. Wren holds it to the wood and paper.

For a moment, the fire will not catch. Perhaps the paper will smolder and smoke will brush the sky and that will be that. For a moment, everyone—Calla, too—holds their breath.

And in an instant, the same way a person dies, the fire catches. It rises. Its brightness joins the day's.

Roger stands, takes his daughter's hand in his. The lighter fluid smell, sharper than gasoline, fills his nose. "At the end of the long night," he says, "Edna St. Cloud was still in the world. She was more of the world than ever before. Her story entwined with the story of death and dying and life and light. Her fire would touch countless lives. A torch for every girl brave enough to fight. It was a story of survival. As is every story that goes on being told."

They watch the fire for a little while. And then, separately or in pairs, they return to the house. The fire burns into late morning. The night is done.

SEVENTEEN

"YOU CAN STILL see the fire out there," James tells Heather, one faltering finger to the window. "Well, you could a moment ago."

"Babe, let's go to sleep."

"You keep on sleeping. I'm too wound up."

"I don't want to miss anything else," she says.

"There's nothing to miss. It's over—until next year." He kisses her. "Thanks for coming. I needed you."

"You would've been fine without me here."

"It's not that."

He kisses her harder now. An animal need awakens in him and, in turn, awakens in her.

"IT ALWAYS ENDS so quickly," Edna says as she sheds her clothes. Roger sits, still dressed, on the bed's edge.

"You were plenty worked up not so long ago," he says.

"Well, it doesn't feel quick in the moment. But it'll never be as bad as it was before we met. You remember the first night I spent in your hotel room? We were up half the night and it was still the best sleep I'd had since—that night."

"Edna, I've been thinking."

"I'm sorry I was being so silly about Wren before, love. You know what it's like: the 31st rolls around and I'm seeing my brother's face in the burnt toast, in the leaves on the trees."

"Edna. Eddie."

"I took the most wonderful photos of her tonight. Our sharp little bird."

"Edna, I've been sleeping with Diana Cutter."

ON THE TV, two girls face off, knives at the ready. Eager to find that the worst is true. In bed, Heather and James pull aside their pajamas, too impassioned or too tired to get undressed. Heather is awake; she bites James's shoulder as he enters her. James bites back—her shoulder, her neck, her lip. He draws blood. She tugs his hair, angles him deeper into her. Not the rote fucking they've learned in four years of love and practice, but something fresh. The way you fuck when you have a new body.

"Oh, Jamie," she says. "Oh, Jamie, Jamie, Jamie."

"DIDN'T YOU HEAR me?" Roger asks. There is a terrible finality to the telling. Words tattooed on the early morning. At least it is done. Edna will be furious, will tell him to go, and then he'll go. "I've been sleeping with Diana. Every time I go to California."

Edna in her pajamas now, straightening the bed around him. There are always more wrinkles to smooth. More imperfections to sand away. "I know that, Roger. I've known for months. It doesn't matter, don't you see? We have the house. We have the morning. The whole family, together again."

"You're tired, you don't know what you're saying."

"I'm the least tired I've ever been, dear heart. Everything is going wonderfully."

Horribly, irreparably, Roger knows that she means this. It is not merely for Wren that he must leave; it is for Edna too. So that they all may look honestly at their lives and decide what will come the next day, and the next.

"Eddie, I'm going to be with her."

She stops patting the bedspread, hands out like a burglar about to be frisked. "For how long?"

"A while."

"A month?" Edna says. "Two?"

"A while, I said."

"But you're coming back."

"Edna . . ."

"And you decided this when?"

"Just now," Roger says.

"Now. Tonight, of all nights."

"It isn't tonight anymore, Ed. It's only another day."

Slowly, very slowly, Edna sinks. A hiss as she drags over the bed, oozing then across the floor, not at all like a woman stabbed.

HEATHER IS ATOP him now, grinding her cunt against him. The heat of his cock inside her like it is a part of her. There is only pleasure. There is only sensation. James whimpers—he does not want to come yet.

"That's good," Heather says. "That's so very, very good."

"Yes."

"You're so good, Jamie. You're a good girl."

"Yes."

⋆ ⋆ ⋆

EDNA SITS UP.

"No," she says.

"It doesn't have to mean anything, Edna. Doesn't have to cheapen—"

"No."

"We'll talk about it when we've slept. We're exhausted."

Edna inhales sharply, readying a scream.

BUT BEFORE SHE can make a sound, their bedroom door flies open to the dawn-soaked hall beyond. And Wren's door opens its mouth so that the girl, sleeping at last, can be seen on her tongue-colored bed. Calla's avatar stands before the vault; with the volume turned all the way up, she can just hear a sound coming from its closed door, a sound like breathing. She jumps as her bedroom door slams (*I'm waiting for you to let me in*) as every door slams. A sound like applause. James's door opens on his and Heather's twisted forms: spent and radiant. Behind an anonymized span of wall, there is the faint thump of a door hitting brick and plaster. The doors to the bathrooms, the basement, the darkroom, the piano room—all open. And the front door. The back door. The garage. The house opened to the day like a body ripe with wounds. Birdsong is filling the halls. The warm wind that presages Virginia summer. And from outside, it is possible to hear Edna let loose that great breath she's drawn, shouting:

"He's here! He's here!"

INTERMISSION

THE MONSTER SPEAKS

WHAT WOULD YOU want?

I could tell it like a choose-your-own-adventure: turn to page 7 if this, to page 20 if that. I could tell it like a murder ballad—Pretty Polly's knife in Willie's heart. I could tell it like a fairy tale. A girl walks into the deep dark woods and never looks back; these woods are her home. I could tell it to you for a thousand nights and you could draw a thousand conclusions and each one would be wrong.

What would you want? The machine dreams for you.

Listen: I am five years old when I first speak. My twin reads to me every day and performs in the small scenes our parents write. I go to therapists, and I do not speak. When at last I find words, I echo the performances. I say, *Strike flat the thick rotundity of the world!* I say, *I resume and concurrently simultaneously for reasons unknown to shrink and dwindle in spite of the tennis.* My parents trot me out at social occasions and say one day I will be a great actor.

My father is a spider-saver, a poetry reader; a whisperer, not a shouter. My mother is a carpenter—they met in the scene shop's sawdust and pine-scent. She could have built a house if we did not already have this one. My twin is—my twin is—my twin is—

What would you want? A series of sequential events, a system of equations that you can solve for *x* and *y*? I never try on the dress.

Later, much later, I wake to blinding light, unable to move my hands, and yell for my mother and father. I yell for my twin and James and even Calla. I yell, at last, for anyone who will listen: God and the Devil, the universe and sky. A nurse with a syringe of sedative. No one comes, and I remember the silence. The limits of language. You call a bear by its name and it descends on your town. You call for the mother who loved you and you're alone in restless torment. By this time the deed is done but—why not?—perhaps this will be explanation enough for you.

YOU CAN MAKE a doll from anything. You can stack two balls of bread and make a face with your thumbnail. You can crumple paper into the tangled form of a body. You can swap and add up these pieces. It is vital to make new bodies. It is years before I learn this.

It is the expectation in our family that we learn some artistic skill. We are eight years old when my twin finds hers. Our father's squat Canon camera is the remnant of an era when he was not a playwright and might have become anyone. My twin tromps around our yard with the camera, snaring out-of-focus birds between branches. She captures the slant of light on our bedroom doors, dust in the afternoon air, and the dark uncertainty backstage before a play begins. My twin finds a light meter at a charity shop and for a while takes it everywhere. As though the sacred numerology of f-stops were the key to Heaven.

She captures the bustle of our parents in the kitchen. They cook together, listening to the late, age-marbled voice of Billie Holiday. Without a word, our father hands our mother an egg. They cook, sometimes, each with an arm around the other, stirring or frying with their free hand. A Platonic body made whole.

When my twin grows tired of these practiced candids, I become her model. It seems a great privilege to me to help her. It is the promise of twinhood—that each of us will understand the other. That, having entered the world together, we will have twice as much life.

What would you want? What would any of us want except to please the people we share the Earth with?

She commands me: Plant your hands. Turn your head. Chin up. I have no idea where she learned to do this; she does not take lessons as I later will. I am a good model—happy to hold a position as she adjusts the focus and exposure. I have often felt the grip of invisible hands about me, moving my body without my will. Now I am my twin's doll to position. I may lie crumpled on the floor for years and I will never hurt.

Our parents coo and cry over the images. They buy her art books: Leiter, Arbus, Leibovitz. She becomes better versed in the art, more demanding in how she poses me. My head hangs over the side of the couch until my vision blurs. Water pours over my face, half drowning me. I'm happy to be told how to be.

But I don't want to see the photos. Despite the odyssey of development—film traded for negatives, contact sheets, prints—they hold too much of me. It isn't like looking in a mirror at all. It is like visiting some past life in a dream and finding it immutable. No matter how loud you scream, you cannot make the image turn away.

My parents hang my sister's portraits around the house. When they catch me, some midnight, clumsily scratching out my own face (pen squeaking over the glass; the photo beneath unbothered) they think it mere jealousy. I believe that's when they know there is something wrong with me. My mother is pregnant with our younger sister a few months later.

★ ★ ★

WHAT WOULD YOU want?

I AM TEN when I find the first piece of wood. I wander the forest behind our house and the fallen branch calls out to me. Something dead and waiting for rot; something I might save by shaping it. I find my first knife in the basement, property of some ancestral St. Cloud. When I carve a face—no one's face, a woman's—my parents are relieved. My lessons with Mr. Catten begin soon after.

The first thing Mr. Catten does on meeting me is flip my hands over to study my palms. Reading my future, I think, only half wrong.

They're soft, he says. *How old're you?*

I'm ten.

We are on his front porch. My mother has dropped me here and returned home to write. I will learn my craft as my parents practice theirs. There is a splintered rocking chair, peeling slate paint. There is a pile of dusty bricks—the foundation for some project abandoned before it began.

Look at mine. There are rough calluses, a scar crossing his lifeline. *Will you let yours harden? Knot and gnarl the way old wood does?*

I have been teased. I have been skipped over at recess sports or tackled into the mud. I am not funny or good at drawing. I am smart, but no smarter than my twin. She spends our school years inching away from our natural-born intimacy.

Doll-making lets me shape a life. I choose how the body's puzzle pieces are assembled. If I have to let the dolls change my body as I change theirs, so be it. Even if I were a different child—the right sort of boy or girl—what am I going to say to this strange man except: *Yes, of course.*

Mr. Catten's house is full of puppets. Marionettes hang on every wall the way art patrons must hang up their collections.

Their blank-faced bodies are costumed in organdy and crushed velvet. Some stand free throughout the room: holding a chrome platter where you might place a drink or, I later learn, cut a line of cocaine; slumped on the edge of bookshelves, a legion of dejected lovers and clowns. One puppet, the stuff of many nightmares, scales the couch's back.

Don't be too impressed. Mr. Catten's voice comes somewhere from under a walrus mustache, and because my own father is clean-shaven, I think the mustache must give the voice its gravel. *I didn't make them,* he says. *They're my wife's.*

She has long been out of the picture. Only her puppets remain.

MY EARLIEST LESSONS are in seeing.

Everything in life, Mr. Catten tells me, can be cut from anything else. From the marble of Michelangelo's *David* you could make a thousand tiny horrors.

He cuts up my work to prove this. The first real doll I make is a clumsy Cinderella. Wavering lines of maple give the impression of hair, a dress. Only the hands are noteworthy: the careful curve of each finger, the slight dip of her nails. Mr. Catten compliments and critiques, takes up his own knife and cuts away pieces of the wooden girl. He reduces her to a hunchbacked hag, one crooked finger reaching for an invisible sun.

There you go, he says, passing me the wooden witch's rough body. *Make that beautiful.*

It's too small, I say. *There's nothing left to cut away.*

Give it a try.

I'm right. It breaks to pieces under my knife.

Try again, he says. Taking my hand in his, guiding my knife across the pieces. His touch is gentle and firm. *Look at what hides behind the wood's blank face. There is little difference between beauty and disgust. A slash through the cheek. A bulb of bone pressing the flesh. There are no static things; it is a matter of how we remake them. How we put the pieces together. You must learn to chase the ugliness, chase the beauty—whichever it is you wish to bring into the world.*

HE TEACHES ME carving, and sewing, and the use of modeling clay. There are hours spent in silence but for a termite feast of slivered wood hitting the floor. If there is a gift Mr. Catten gives me, it is this freedom. I have lived as a doll, moved from room to room by invisible hands. I have been a puzzle whose pieces can be forced to fit but do not effortlessly notch together. Here, I learn control. I learn to shape a joint, to hide a flaw. And I learn to sit in silence—to chase the beauty, together.

I come in one afternoon to find him before the television. On-screen, a beautiful red-haired woman dances through phantasmagoric carnivals, through a pas de deux with a windswept newspaper. She keeps dancing and dancing; a pair of ruby ballet slippers carries her through these steps until she beautifully collapses and dies. And then, somehow, the film keeps going. I do not move, afraid of disturbing the spell. The woman loves a young composer, but her director will not work with a woman in love. She is torn between them—between love and art. She fights with her lover. She howls in despair. At the film's end, she is hit by a train and dies.

At last I speak. *Can we watch the dance scene again?*

Mr. Catten rewinds the tape. We watch the woman come to life, dancing backward through Europe's elaborate halls. When the scene ends, I ask him to replay it again. Normally the lesson would have ended by now, but he obliges. There is amusement in his face and something else. Something I do not know the name for.

Why do you like this scene so much? he asks as it begins again.

I don't have to think about my answer. *It's beautiful.*

But she dies. She dies onstage and in real life.

She dies for art.

Mr. Catten shakes his head. *A stupid thing to die for.*

I AM FOURTEEN the second time I see a naked body. I am always in the forest now, looking for bits of wood that interest me. Mr. Catten disdains these findings, says they aren't good wood. But there is pleasure in the random and the damaged. There are always more castoffs to save from the world's rot.

And the family is better when I am gone. My twin waits in the living room for the light to move a few centimeters. Calla, with her trunk of costumes, dresses up James. My parents' typewriter tap dance, a new play every six months, read out to us over the dinner table. And here I am. The branches make cathedral arches.

I am looking at the trees and so do not see the boy until I nearly trip over him. He sits on a sturdy log I have noticed before—even climbed over. There is a magazine open on his bare thighs, his cock laid across it.

Hey, man, he says. *The log is occupado, capisce? Come back in ten.*

What?

You know what, make it fifteen. The boy makes no move to hide his nudity. *I think, with enough time, Miss November and I can make something really special.*

I'm—

The boy's eyes linger on my eyes, lips, lashes. *You are a boy*, he says, *right? You're not some kind of crazy dyke who's going to cut off my dick?*

Yes. I mean, I'm a boy. I'm— I say my name.

Yeah, yeah, I didn't ask your life story. Now, beat it. Or rather— don't. He laughs.

I walk only far enough to leave his sight. There is birdsong and the crackle of deer on dead leaves, but I hear nothing from the boy's direction. There is a nice piece of oak lying seven feet off—a log that someone cut and forgot to take—but I don't claim it. I think of the love my parents have—too much love, surely too much. I think about nudity, and how my twin strips me for her camera. Poses me with her friend. I think about killing someone with a gun, and how impersonal it must be. The bullet could fall from anywhere. It could be a stone sailing out of Heaven.

His voice comes back like a church bell: *Log's all yours!*

He is zipping up his shorts. He stows the magazine in the log—hollow, I see now.

I'd shake hands, he says, *but, well, I don't recommend it. Name's Patrick.*

I repeat my name, and he smiles.

I know, he says.

You don't usually run into people out here, he says. *Or I never have. Sometimes I thought I was the only one who knew. Just me and the girls, a little paler every time it rains.*

Did you know, he says, *that Saint Nicholas is the patron saint of hookers?*

Like Santa Claus?

Some people think it's Saint Vitalis but that's bullshit. It's definitely Saint Nicholas. He raised money to pay some girls so they could get married instead of being whores. Patrick smiles. Gap teeth, shaggy straw-colored hair in his eyes. *If I was a girl*, he says, *I'd take the money and still sell my pussy.*

Anyway, smell ya later, he says. *If you steal any of the magazines I will know and I will fuck you up.*

A long time passes between when he disappears into the trees and when I look inside the log.

Weeks later, the first time I suck Patrick off, his come is salty and smells like bread dough. This sex is never quite right for me. I want to be like the magazines' shallow images—the soft bodies that fill the pages, the curve of hip and tit. The empty eyes. The spurt of come on chin and face. Bargain bin sex. McDonald's sex. But all I ever have is the pale image of the real.

SOMETIMES WHEN I am failing to sleep, the ceiling goes transparent black. A dusting of stars comes down to me and swims through the darkness like sparks off a fire. I brush them with my fingers and they clack together like beads. It is a swirling, golden horn of light and it belongs to everyone. There isn't any darkness in the universe, not really, not if you look closely enough.

Sometimes, when I look in the mirror, there is a camera watching me from behind it. I mouth: *Fuck you. I'll fuck you up.* It's a weak imitation of Patrick's swagger. I know that whoever watches is not frightened.

I never make a dollhouse for the same reason I never keep a diary. There are people who can keep material traces of their desires and there are people who cannot.

Instead, I pencil floor plans on graph paper and shuttle dolls through these silver houses. I draw enough sprawling rooms for four games of Clue. A rectangle can be a bed. A different rectangle is a bookshelf. A circle is a glass coffeepot. My dolls do not talk to one another. They face the walls. They lie in bed at night and their eyes do not close.

They used to live lives. Used to touch, to talk over the dinner table. To wink, blink, wander the graphite grounds looking for arrowheads. But as I grow older, they run out of things to say. They are happier for it.

I am too afraid to keep my pencil houses. When I finish playing, I tear them up. I flush them down the toilet, or burn them in the sink, or eat them a piece at a time. There is a house inside me.

All my joy is in gifting faceless wood with expression. No wonder that history is full of tales of dolls come to life. It is a real power, like that of childbirth, to sculpt a body from the inanimate.

WHAT WOULD YOU want?

FOR A WHILE, when we begin middle school, my twin has no need of me as a model. She finds a new subject in Beatrice Fulton.

Everyone who knows Beatrice finds her beautiful, though what she is is merely full of life. We are in seventh-grade English together, and she makes pornographic malapropisms of every title assigned (e.g., *The Cunt of Monte Fisto*) that so distress our teacher that he kicks her out of class. After that moment, she never pushes too hard again. She is always seeking limits.

This is the spirit she brings to my sister's photographs. She is put through the familiar contortions—nose and mouth shoved into the dirt, lying with water poured over her face. When the photos come back, her expression is defiant of the world, and God, and the body's natural bounds.

It is Beatrice who first suggests my twin ought to strip her subjects naked. There is a darkroom now—a cramped bathroom in the basement with blacked windows and a red light bulb. If her film were still going through one-hour photo shops, perhaps things would have ceased here. The Fultons may not have allowed Beatrice to come to our house anymore. My sister may have given up her camera entirely. And I may have—may have not—may have—but what does it matter now? What would you want? Here is what happens.

I am in my own basement workshop carving toys for baby James. I will make a box of noisemakers: a rattle of wooden beads, interlocking rings that clack when shaken, a croaking frog-shaped guiro. Recently I made a goose call, with which I hide around the house. When I let out a long, happy honk, wee James will toddle in, looking for the goose. I always tell him it has just left and that we will go find it together.

I am in my basement workshop and the door unsticks, unfamiliar footsteps tramp down the stairs. I set aside my tools, my rough wooden rings, and wait with a hand on each knee. I have grown longer recently; I try to keep myself contained.

Your sister wants you, Beatrice says. She searches the workshop. A dozen doll faces watch her. She doesn't tease or ask about the work. She is a judge before a crowded court.

Okay, I say, and stand.

Do you ever know what she's thinking? Beatrice asks. *Twin telepathy?*

Why don't you ask her?

What makes you think I haven't?

We are the same height. Her hair falls darkly over her forehead and shoulders in wide ringlets. Her breath is rich with the smell of cinnamon gum; she must have spit it out just before coming down.

Of course I do, I lie.

What does she think about?

She thinks you're a beautiful subject.

Beatrice's worry cracks; there's a wry smile beneath it.

Fucking liar, she says. *You don't know anything.*

On the lawn waits my sister with her camera. She poses us in imitation of Grant Wood's gothic couple; Beatrice holds a knobby stick in place of a pitchfork. My sister takes some shots, moves here and there.

It is pretense. She shakes her head after each. She says, *Take your clothes off.*

What?

All artists use nude models, Beatrice says. *What's the matter, you scared?*

Don't antagonize him, Bea.

But she doesn't need words. She is already pulling her shirt over her head, undoing the snap at the front of her pants. Her clothes pile on the grass, remnants of a raptured body. Her skin is so white it, like the moon, seems to borrow no light, to glow from within.

I cannot breathe. I have no lungs or heart. I can't expose my ugliness in a world accustomed to such beauty.

And then I have a vision, as clear and real as the stars coming out of the sky. I am a proper twin, beautiful as every girl on Earth. I take the legs of this one, the hips of this other, the hands and breasts. A knife brings out the beauty within me and the world is my home. I pull my shirt off in the same way, and it is only when I feel the early autumn air that I remember.

I stop, half out of my shirt.

Roland, my sister says, and I flinch. I am disgusting where they are pure. I extrude where they dip. There is already a pale felt of hair over my lip and waist. I am frozen. I cannot stop. I strip.

(And where are our parents? Propped on the couch reading Caryl Churchill in alternating voices. Or they are practicing the steps of a waltz, dressed in Victorian costumes. Or they doze with our siblings, those symbols of enduring love who still rarely sleep through the night. We are not free through choice, but because they cannot keep their attention off each other.)

I never try on the dress. I am never alone in my house. I never see the photos from that day.

We are Adam and Eve in the garden: Beatrice with a candle grin forces an apple into my mouth. Water gems our arms and legs as we wade into the stream behind the house. Beatrice touches me on command and pulls away after the shutter falls. She gives me the same wry grin. *Liar,* she'd said. *Fucking liar.* I look to the sun to save me—the wild, ordinary starlight that washes over every person who's ever lived. Every person we are, and every person we might have been.

WHAT WOULD YOU want? What would you have done?

PERHAPS IT'S TO prove something that Patrick offers himself to me. And to prove something else (I will fail in this) that I accept.

The next time we meet his pants are zipped. Waiting for me.

Hey there, space cadet, he salutes. *Kept the log warm for you.*

I do not know how to be. I could carve this log into a beautiful chest, decorate it with the wooden bodies of nude women. It would save the magazines, those girls of living flesh, from the rain and sun. Patrick looks up at me. He wears three rings on his fingers. Real silver, I think.

Let's see what's on the menu today, eh, boy-o?

Patrick pulls magazines from the log, like a magician's scarves all come undone. *Titter* and *Fling* and *Soul Mates. Venus* and *Cloud.* Here are his favorite girls. Seams up their stockings, PVC boots, peep-toe shoes. What must it be like to stand before a camera that loves you, so beautiful that people will pay you for it? To stand in the middle of a crowd—a train platform, a theater lobby—and know that every man in the place wants your softness? It must come off of these women like nuclear radiation.

Aren't you Catholic? I ask.

The fuck are you talking about?

The saints, I explain.

No, I'm not fucking Catholic. Whatta question.

We meet here weekly. We sit, and look, and he comes in my mouth. I love these meetings in the woods. It's a simple exchange, the grace of my body meeting his. I will never have the love I want, but these moments are close, close enough.

After, we lie, not touching, in the slant beams of forest sun. Because he has to say something, or because he enjoys sharing, he tells me about saints.

Saint Simeon, who sat atop a pillar for thirty-five years to escape the needs of others. Boys brought him goat's milk and bread up there, which proves something, I think, about need.

Saint Lucy had her eyes gouged out.

Saint Teresa had visions of ecstatic penetration.

Saint Agatha had her breasts cut off. Saint Wilgefortis grew a beard. These women would do anything to dodge marriage. They would save their sex for God.

My favorite is Saint Margaret. After she converted to Christianity, Margaret's father forced her to leave home. She was tortured and imprisoned for rejecting a pagan's sexual advances. The devil, in the form of a dragon, came to her in prison and swallowed her whole. Inside his belly, the cross Margaret carried turned into a sharp silver sword, and she cut her way out.

As I drift toward sleep I think, I am in the belly of the dragon. By the time I wake, Patrick will have gone back to a home I never see. I am in the belly of the dragon, and I will cut my way out.

MR. CATTEN CARVES misshapen women. Their breasts are uneven, their faces sour. Even the girlish among them are like fairy-tale witches—ready at the drop of a pointed hat to gobble a child or put a maiden in a coma.

He passes these to me during our Monday lessons. *Make this beautiful*, he says. I am fourteen by the time I learn how. My knife is steadied by his hand on mine. Rough fingers on my soft skin. One crooked figure becomes deer stooping to drink from a pond. Another, a bowed choir of lilies of the valley. In turn, he makes them again into hags. Back and forth they go, from his knife to mine, until they are cut to nothing. Women become unrecognizable stumps, saving themselves from—what?

The thing you must understand, he says, *is that a doll has only the spirit you put into it. A puppet has its own soul.*

He met his wife at a trade show; they'd collaborated for a while. She was the better craftsperson. She'd had other reasons for leaving. He lost his drive for doll-making but has gone on carving automatically, a single-purpose machine. When I ask him where he keeps his finished work, he gestures with his chin at the fireplace.

Only thing for them, he says. *Purified by fire.*

We keep watching *The Red Shoes*; the ballet sequence two, three, four times. I don't have to ask. We both love to watch Moira Shearer dance. No one has ever been so free. It is an impossible thing, to be a body like this. I carve ballet dancers out of birch, and Mr. Catten reduces them to ghouls.

One day he queues up *Peeping Tom*. Here, too, is Moira Shearer, dancing to the point of death. Here, too, she is put in an impossible position by the men making art of her. The film's hero is Carl Boehm, an anxious photographer who videotapes women as he murders them. *Whatever I photograph I always lose*, he says to the downstairs neighbor he is in love with. She is nothing. She is forgettable. It is Moira Shearer who is the point. Boehm places her, chalks her mark on the soundstage floor. But she dances for herself. The drums are jazzy. *Mind if I warm up?* she asks.

She throws limbs left and right, wraps her arms about her as though embracing a lover. Every step, every spin disregards Boehm's camera. She is freer still than in *The Red Shoes*. Her body moves as if it alone defines space. As if, without her, there would be only formless color and immeasurable distance.

(If I were. If I could be. Anyone at all. I could be.)

I do feel alone in front of it, she says of the camera. *I suppose stars never do.*

They feel alone without it, Boehm replies. *The great ones feel alone all the time.*

The horns pick up and she goes on dancing. The scene is being set for her death, and she dances still. This is girlhood. This is a dream. At the soundstage door, a title card tells us: "THE WALLS ARE CLOSING IN." NO ADMITTANCE. The music rewinds, but the dancing is done. Moira Shearer stands on her mark, trapped in the frame of Boehm's camera.

Wouldn't it be better if I just did my number? she asks. And Boehm shakes his head.

The camera's tripod becomes a weapon. A knife at her throat as the film runs through. Moira Shearer is done dancing; her dead body will be found, later, folded up in a trunk. Crumpled like an unstrung puppet.

In my room, I try her steps. I spin, throw my limbs, bob my head. I wrap myself in my arms. Her arms. It is her hair I run my fingers through. And it is me in the camera's crosshairs, captured as I die in an effortless body.

I wish I could borrow the film from Mr. Catten. After waking from a dream of princess turned hag turned fawn, I could sneak down the creaky stairs and watch her dance in the living room. I could watch until morning's light. But I cannot bear to ask for it. Instead, I am left with the memory of his fingers' weight. The guiding pressure.

I tell Mr. Catten about my siblings. James is old enough that the world's stories stick in his brain. He and Calla act out scenes of her devising. She is always the princess, and James, the evil witch.

I never tell him about my sister's photos, but I tell him about the freedom we have—or what we call freedom. We entertain ourselves. We spend our days on our art and our games.

I tell him that the other day, James fell and scraped his knee; our father did not look up from his reading as he told James where to find bandages. His howls rang through the house. Mr. Catten doesn't say anything to that, only puts his hand on mine.

You interested in any girls at school? he asks me.

Girls?

Or boys? he adds.

The magazines in the log sometimes feature men fucking men. I find no correspondence between what they do and what I do with Patrick.

No, I tell him. *There's no one.*

You should be, he says. *It'll make you happier than this.*

I AM FOURTEEN, fifteen, and the invisible hands that move me are larger. I am thrust into rooms with no idea how I got there, how to leave. I wait for the fingers to envelop me completely.

My twin has no trouble. She is the eye. She is commander and killer.

She poses me and Beatrice naked in the dirt. *God*, my twin says, *when is the last time you showered? Can't you shave that little pedo stache?*

But we are twins. There has been some mistake. My softness should match hers. I should be able to change—a shift in the eyes' focus, a different path through the woods at night. You should be able to carve a body the way you carve a doll. Cut away the ugliness, chase the beauty. With a knife's tip, you should piece together something like a self. I am right, I know I'm right, and my righteousness should be a sword. Every mirror is a mechanical eye. A camera buried behind two-way glass traps me in its cross-hairs, kills me daily.

My body, thick and real, sinks into the earth. I cannot tell my twin about the mirror. Cannot explain the everydayness of it.

I AM THIRTEEN the first time Beatrice comes to my room.

She often sleeps at our house. She and my twin stay up late listening to Beach Boys records. I spend the evening teaching James to play chess. I carved the pieces myself, one for each member of the family. Our parents are king and queen. The bishops are my twin; the knights, Calla; the rooks, our home. And the pawns are all little James. Sixteen child faces, hair cut into a bowl. He does not like the rules. In time we have an all-out battle: black against white, good against ill, family against family against family.

When I settle down to sleep, the battle still rages behind my eyes. Pieces fall, the living and the dead in rigid repose. James asks why there are no pieces that look like me.

Hey there, says Beatrice. Standing by my bed, sudden as a ghost.

Hello, I say. She says nothing, only looms over me. *Are you having trouble sleeping?*

It's my birthday.

Happy birthday.

Beatrice stumbles over to the desk. A handful of figures wait there for varnish. She picks up a wolf dressed in grandmother clothes. Its hinged stomach can open to reveal a tiny red-caped girl and shriveled old woman within.

You're a fucking weirdo, aren't you, Roland?

I am, I say.

Not like other boys.

She drops the wolf, and its neck cracks. She is beside me again, breath bready with wine. She kisses me hard. Her tongue curls behind my teeth. I picture a snail searching for a new home. I picture her disappearing into me, breathing when I breathe. Her hands puppeting mine.

You don't know what it's like, she says, *to love a boy who doesn't love you. You can't be rejected because you don't know how to love.*

I am not so naïve as to imagine she means me. I never learn which of the numberless alternates she loves. Which of the boys like other boys. I'm all she can trap.

She kisses me again, and I let her. She does not care how I respond.

I'm going to teach you, she says. *I'm going to give you the thrill of your faggy little life.*

She strips off her underwear and lowers her cunt to my face. I understand the demand of warm and wet. But I keep my mouth shut to her. She slaps my cheek.

Fucking open sesame, you little freak. It's my birthday.

Wanting only for this to end, I do as she says. She grinds against me for some minutes. Her breath heavy above me. I think about the woods in spring. The cathedral arches broken, tree limbs shed beneath winter's ice. I think of the beauty hidden in each of Mr. Catten's hags, and the horror beneath that beauty. The collision of two bodies makes it hard to know which is yours.

And then Beatrice's hand wraps around the base of my sex. I throw her off. She makes a heap on the floor, long T-shirt barely covering her.

She is smiling when she stands. Her teeth almost glow in the moonlight.

Too much excitement for you, huh? She wipes her mouth and spits on the pillow. In the morning, I will find blood there. *Tell me happy birthday.*

Happy birthday.

She disappears into the black night.

★ ★ ★

ALL THIS HAPPENS before I meet Patrick. I never associate the two acts. One is soft and golden. One is cracked wood and blood.

I never see the pictures. I am never alone.

There is no guessing when Beatrice will return. Some nights she stays with Edna and I sleep undisturbed. Some nights she only studies me like a lump of uncarved wood. And sometimes she climbs onto my mouth, barely allowing me breath, slapping me into compliance. She never tries to touch me at the root again.

She sneers at me in the high school halls, laughs about my uncouth body in the cafeteria and gym. There are no gay people in our school, let alone people like me.

What else could I deserve? What else could you want?

There were early days when my twin and I were close. We built mud palaces in the backyard. Ate ice creams the size of our faces. There was our father at the piano, leading us in show songs. Our parents wrote parts for us in their plays; we played the same character on alternating nights. One watched in the wings while the other spoke, and when we fell asleep, we could not remember who had taken the stage that night.

I could have been any man. I could have been a hermit at the known world's edge. I could have thrived in the era of martyrs and fools. I could have been a saint, insane and kind. There is little distance between saint and monster. It is a matter of timing, I think, and faith, and that's all. But in this life, I have no place. The closest I come is the forest.

I AM FOURTEEN, fifteen, sixteen. Patrick tells me about Saint Christina, who died and saw the full scale of Heaven and Hell. A hundred million souls, he tells me, packed into a grimy, too-small room. Mildew in the tiles and lockers no one knows the combination to.

He tells me about Saint Oran. Each day the walls of a new chapel fell, so Saint Oran consented to be buried alive in the foundation. Then the chapel stood. *And one day*, Patrick says, *he stuck his head up to tell people there was no Heaven and no Hell.*

So which is it? I say.

What do you mean?

They can't both be true.

Yeah, they can, he says. *Why would anyone make them up?*

He tells me that when you die, your body becomes a home—to worms, bacteria, beetles. *Grass roots deep inside you*, he says, *and reaches up toward Heaven.* And making a house—any house—is an act of love. You have to imagine the future that will come within its walls. You need a room for sleep and a room for cooking and one for fucking and one for illness. *When Martians land*, he says, *and go on package tours of our houses, will they know by looking what each room is for? Will their bodies fit in our chairs and beds and bathtubs?*

Sixteen years old and I still swallow my paper dollhouses. I wonder if those worlds carry on inside of me. Stories in a book no one is reading.

You never talk, Patrick says.

What?

You never say what you're thinking. Hiding away behind that glorious fucking mouth of yours. He's smiling. I don't know what to say. *What do you like?* he asks.

I have never told him about the dolls, the house, my goose game with James. I do not mention Beatrice, or Mr. Catten. And Patrick tells me nothing of real life. I don't know where he lives or what his last name is. I only know about the saints. They dance above our heads, shedding light over us as we doze in every weather.

I like movies, I say.

No kidding? A cinephile, huh? He's propped up, now, on the porn log. *We should go sometime.*

To the movies?

Yeah. Not like a fucking date or anything. But it blows going to them alone. You always end up with too much popcorn. His smile does not fade. *How about it, boy-o?*

OUR PARENTS' PLAYS are performed by local theater troupes, workshopped in the capital or in northern New York. Every opening night, my siblings and I are in the audience. We watch life fill the stage—born out of our parents' love and labored hours. This is what our mother and father have done instead of watching us. This is what they train us for—an artist's life of inhuman distance. Voices fill these shows as they never do our home.

I must be thirteen the year I see myself onstage. I can't recall the show's name. There was a family, a disordered mess of rooms. There was a house threatened with condemnation. James and Calla are still too young to sit through the whole thing; my twin and I take turns taking them to the lobby. Little James naps against my shoulder; Calla races from one end of the building to the other. The pleasure, at that age, of moving.

It is when I return to the theater that I recognize myself. A lisping boy onstage holds a Raggedy Andy doll. He explains that he has never been good at understanding people, but that he understands dolls. People laugh at this. Dolls' expressions do not change, the boy says. Their touch is reliable. As he speaks, he peels off Raggedy Andy's clothes, revealing the unsexed white body beneath.

He is offensive. He is pathetic. I feel my twin's stare. There are so many eyes in the room.

I begin to doubt. Is this who I am? Am I meant to learn from this, to change? My parents knew I would be in the audience.

Either it is a message for me or I am wrong about everything. He could be another boy, from another family, in another town. I want to crawl onto the stage and slap him until his pasty face looks sunburned. I want to shake him, shout him down. I want to show him the woods—the safety of the branches, the peace of the light.

As the play goes on, the boy grows quieter. His mother rips his dolls to pieces and burns them in the fireplace. Eventually the house is bulldozed with him inside it.

Everybody stands to applaud so tragic an end.

MY SKILLS PLATEAU, but every Monday finds me at Mr. Catten's house. I use his power tools to make puzzle boxes, whistles, and rings. Beyond Patrick and James, he is the only person who enjoys my company. He lets me sit in companionable silence and work another body into being.

These days there's usually a Tom Waits record on the turntable. Mr. Catten sometimes sings along in his bell-clear baritone: "*I was always so impulsive, I guess that I still am. All that really mattered then was that I—was a man.*"

Sometimes he cuts a line of cocaine on the puppet-held platter. Sometimes he offers me a bump. It makes my body too much, my blood too red.

I do not plan to ask him the question. It slips. *Do you believe in God?* I ask.

God?

Yes.

You're asking me if I believe in God?

I wouldn't know how to answer either. Patrick has taught me: there was a time of miracles, and that time has passed. But surely it could begin again. We might all be touched by God's light at any moment.

Look around, he says. *Does this look like a life rewarded for devotion? Does this look like I got everything I ever wanted?*

I want to tell him that there both are and aren't a Heaven and a Hell. That there are saints that will ferry our souls to the sublime forever. I would walk across a trillion miles of darkness to free myself. I would make any cross into a silver sword.

All I actually know is that I am in the dragon's belly. That I am responsible, responsible alone, for fighting my way out.

But someone must be able to show me the way. I cannot be the darkness's only wanderer.

BEATRICE'S CUNT ON my face in the darkness. What would it be like to have this power? To touch and be touched at your slightest whim?

Is it working? she asks. *Are you a man yet?*

Sometimes she tells me about the boys who fuck her. She crouches over them in their cars while their fingers worry her jacket's peeling red pleather. *I'm a fucking astronaut*, she says. *I'm on the goddamn moon.*

I don't wonder that she keeps coming to me. Every mirror is an eye. Every bulge of my body is an affront against God. But this closeness, for all its calamity, gives me a moment of pretense: I could be that red-pleather girl. These boys want Beatrice and she wants me and so by some transitive property—

She always spits on my pillow, sometimes my face. *For luck*, she says.

PATRICK IS WAITING outside the movie theater.

Got all dressed up, did you?

For a moment, I don't recognize the joke. I am the girl in the peeling red jacket. I couple furtively in steamed cars. We are just two kids, meeting here as any might.

Patrick's grin gives him away. I am dressed in an everyday polo shirt and loose jeans. He isn't wearing his rings.

We don't get popcorn. We don't touch the whole night. Those days in the woods happened to someone else. But we laugh in the dark, surrounded by kids like us. The movie is stupid and beautiful. Arnold Schwarzenegger has been given memories of a life that isn't his. He goes into a machine that dreams for him. It reminds him of his true self: he is a secret agent. There is something about a rebel group on Mars. By film's end, there are blue skies above the barren planet.

We sit on the curb after. We do not have a ride home, we do not know how to part. In the past, there has always been the safety of the woods.

Do you really think it's that easy? I ask. *To forget who you always were? To become someone else?*

Sure, boy-o. Patrick is distracted, biting his nails. *In fifteen years, maybe twenty. They'll do it every day. You'll get sick of your wife and—* zap*—you'll be given a new one. A whole new set of memories to boot.*

It sounds kind of sinister, I say, *when you put it that way.*

Nothing sinister about it. If you never learned, it wouldn't make any difference.

He kicks a chip bag until the wind takes it. It blows toward the universe's corners but catches against a lamppost.

I've been meaning to ask you something, I say.

You've never asked me a goddamn thing in your life.

I almost ask: What's wrong? It isn't that the movie was a mistake. It isn't this, here and now, or we wouldn't linger. Instead, I say:

Tell me about Saint Cloud.

Saint Cloud? Like Minnesota?

He doesn't know my last name any more than I know his.

Sure, I say. *It's got to be named after someone.*

I've never heard of a Saint Cloud. He spits his bitten-off nails on the tarmac. For luck, I think. *It sounds like a nobody saint. Like the bad guy in an Arnold flick.*

Yeah—okay. My eyes fall. The theater lights are shutting off, and we both have a considerable walk home. *Well, see you later.*

See you, space cadet.

I leave him alone in the mounting dark. The boy with ragged nails. Our movie night either a failed experiment, or a successful one. It's unclear which option is more frightening.

The experiment doesn't matter. I never see Patrick again.

I GO THROUGH phases.

It is my fault (bad timing): I spend hours in the woods, waiting for him.

It is my fault (wrongdoing): I whisper apologies to the leaves that mulch the ground, to the wind-traced clouds. I dream of a flock of crows, each carrying one syllable of my crisis to Patrick, and he arrives beneath my floorboards, whispers soothing words. We will be together as soon as I pry up this rotted wood.

It is my fault (unclean living): I do not imagine another life. I work hard to live in my flesh. There is comfort in the darkness of the dragon's belly. When Beatrice comes at night, I open my mouth gladly for her. She cackles over me. *Getting to like the taste?* She grinds me to a pulp.

It is my fault (lack of penance): I hide in the library, head pressed to the cold beige shelves, and study the lives of the saints. Saint John the Silent, who talked quite a lot. Saint Andrew, who was crucified on an X-shaped cross. Saint Barbara, whose torture-wounds were healed by morning's light. Without Patrick, the saints are horrible. You would be terrified if either their suffering or their miracles happened to someone you knew. It wouldn't make you believe in God. You probably wouldn't believe in anything after that.

I go to the movies as often as I'm able. I look for Patrick's shaggy hair among the darkened rows but find only confederacies of friends, lovers with their heads together. I eat only stale popcorn and drink only syrupy Coke. I am in this desert for forty days, and another forty, and another. I have never been deeper in the dragon's belly; there is no hint of light. There is only applause, and fear.

LOOK, YOU'VE KNOWN all along: at some point it becomes clear that I will kill them. My twin and Beatrice and whoever else I need to. I have been so close to these bodies; if there is a soul, I ought to be able to free it. Flesh should be malleable as wood. Life given or exchanged by the knife's point—as a doll comes to life. If my act is just, I will be rewarded like a saint. If I am unjust then I will be sent to Hell; I am ready—eager—for the suffering.

But I am still sixteen. I have my Monday lessons. Life goes on and on and ends all at once.

We barely carve these days. Mr. Catten puts on other movies—John Carpenter and Ridley Scott. We crack cans of High Life and settle into his couch. This is all that holds me after Patrick is gone.

I thought I'd try puppets, I tell him. *They're a natural next step from dolls.*

No. A sluggish shake of his head. His weedy mustache curls into his mouth. *No, it's a cursed art. Impure. Making a thing with the spark of life. An affront to God.*

You don't believe in God. I'm more daring now. He's the only thing I have like a friend.

I didn't say that. He sips deeply and I follow him. Being tipsy warms the darkness. Boundaries become senseless. On the TV, Kurt Russell lands a military glider on top of the Twin Towers. *What I said was, does this look like devotion's reward?*

The next week, or the week after, I find him already drunk.

What do you want? Mr. Catten asks.

My first beer of the evening hisses open. *What do I want from what?*

From life. The future. If you could have anything, what would it be?

I don't imagine a future, I say.

I expect him to push back, as my parents do when we talk of SATs and college applications. Instead, he nods.

I know what you are, he says. *I know what you want.*

I freeze with my can halfway to my mouth. This man—old, thin, drunk. Lonely as a ghost. I want to say, I am nothing. I am like Patrick, with his arcane knowledge and strange phrases. I am something sacred and something cursed.

Instead I say: *What do you mean?*

Don't worry, he says, *I like it. My wife was a real sport about it for a while. She had a history in the circus. Get all types in there. People who like to be cut open a little. People who like electric shocks. But she never could understand why I loved the girls. Why I'd meet them in the rain, dresses gathered around their cocks.* He laughs, crushes his empty can, pulls a full one from the couch cushions. *They were so beautiful. So eager for my touch. And my wife—how could I explain? It's not that she wasn't enough. Only that the girls were so much more.* The new can hisses. A serpent in the garden.

You'll be such a pretty girl, he says. *My pretty girl.*

I'm not.

I cannot be—

What's that? he says.

I cannot be the darkness's only wanderer.

I'm not going—going to—

Oh sure, sure. Mr. Catten shakes his head again. I see that his fly is open, perhaps has been since before I arrived. His penis is long, thin, and pale; it hangs from him like a fluke. His eyes meet mine, not bothering to question.

And who else do you think will have you? he says.

Such a pretty girl, he says.

I am gone. I look over my shoulder. The porch with its peeling paint. The house with its cast of puppets, its ash of hags and princesses, its lonely ogre. He will lumber along like a bear, knife in hand, no neighbor in sight. He'll descend on me, press himself into my mouth, and—

I am out of breath when I reach home. I slam the door with my back, press to it like a heart presses a rib, and sink. The least breach would be an ending.

Mommy? I call out. *Dad?*

They're at the theater.

Edna watches from the top of the stairs, arms crossed with contempt.

Eddie, come down here. Please.

She sits on the step, still watching. *You look like shit.*

Slowly, so slowly, I move away from the door. I stay on the floor, unwilling to rise.

Something happened, Eddie.

Oh?

I tell her everything I can. I tell her about Mr. Catten. About Beatrice. The great ballooning of my chest, ready to burst. I tell her all of it and in the telling it feels too small. Maybe it is her face.

Maybe it is the air's stillness. There is no shaking door, no seismic event. There is only life. Today, like yesterday and tomorrow. A few hours of light, bordered by dark.

When I finish telling, Edna says, *Is that all?*

You have to believe me.

I do believe you. What I asked was, is that all?

What?

I gotta hand it to Bea, she chuckles, *getting within a yard of your face is fucking freaky. The others are going to lose it when I tell them.*

You can't.

Yes, I can. Her face is shadowed. Some obscure jealousy passing through her. Would it have been different if I told her about Patrick? About the dragon, and the mirror, and the dress?

You have to help me, I say.

Roland, do you know what I have to deal with every goddamn day? She is standing now, making to leave. *Do you know the first time I got catcalled? I was fucking twelve years old.*

But—

I get groped at school, what, twice a week? Scott Wilshire offered me a ride home once and got on the highway going eighty and wouldn't slow down until I jerked him off.

I wince.

Look at you, she says, *you fucking baby. Calling for your mommy because of a cock no one made you suck. Welcome to real life, Rollie.*

She leaves me in my pathetic heap. I don't have the energy to stand, to climb the stairs, to hide. I think she is gone for good. But she returns, Leica in hand.

She says, *Look alive, darling.*

The camera flashes, and my panic is made permanent.

She doesn't deserve it, I think, and there is another flash. She doesn't deserve any of it. The pain or the joy.

Another flash. She runs through a roll of film. If those pictures still linger somewhere, you could make a flip-book of them. See the slow realization dawn.

WHAT WOULD YOU want? How do you learn your wanting? Who could have taught me mine?

Do I do it because of Mr. Catten? Because of Beatrice and Edna and the invisible hands? Do I do it because the age of miracles has ended or because it is just beginning? Yes, all of these. No, none of them. Whatever drives me must be akin to that which brings Beatrice to my room some nights and not others. What drove Mr. Catten. His hand on mine, coaxing forth the dolls' flesh.

What would you want? The choice between killing and dying is no choice at all. One day James will be at a college in the north, writing film reviews for the student paper. He will leave behind the world in which he grew up; he will keep contact with no one from home. Calla will be popular in high school—the only person in our family who truly is. She'll go to Georgetown, a few hours away by train. She'll come home on breaks, send birthday presents to her old clique, do Yankee Swaps at the holidays. And my sister and I, we will carry these wrongs. We will die, the monstrous St. Clouds will die. Let others be our judges.

THE FINAL TIME I go to the movies I know little about the film playing, except that it is meant to be scary. When I see the man on the screen, I don't understand at first. What I think is that his hair and voice are like Patrick's, but he is ugly. He is skinning girls. He hurts them like Beatrice. He traps one in a well and taunts her and tells her to soften herself so that he might one day be soft.

There is another killer in the movie: a man jailed for eating people. But his crime is nothing compared to the real villain's. By the movie's end, the cannibal will be free and the man, the monster—Jame—will be dead.

It takes too long for me to understand—this man with almost my brother's name. This man who is almost my brother. He never makes himself beautiful. Another wanderer in the dark. A monster like me. It is as though a voice of light issues from the screen saying, *This is how you make it through. This is how you make yourself.*

I TAKE THE dress from my sister's closet. She is out with a boy called George, with Beatrice and one of her car boys.

It is not hard to alter the dress. I am good with my hands. I chase the beauty. Cut strips, hem the bottom. I rip stitches here, sew in a panel there. It is the ivory pink of a shell's underside. I hear the life of the house above me: our mother typing in the study, the narrow circuit of my father pacing; Calla and James practicing dance steps. One by one they sleep, and I finish my tailoring. When all is silent and still, I hasten upstairs with the dress in hand. I do not think of discovery until I see James sitting on the stairs, face drawn with sleeplessness.

What is it, little goose? I ask. *Can't sleep?*

He shakes his head.

Bad dream?

Another shake—not a *no*. Only trying to clear a path for thought.

I dreamed the house was on fire, he says.

I smile, reach for him with my free hand. The other holds the dress behind me. *How would a thing like that happen?*

It came up through the ground, he says. *It came up like lava. Like Pompeii.*

Well—

And it fell from the sky. And it came out of the walls like a ghost.

Tell you what, I say. *You go back to sleep, and I'll sit up, and make sure no fire gets in, okay? And if it tries to, you know what I'll do?*

Another shake of his head. His eyes are beginning to close. Already he's taken my hand, and lets me lead him to his room.

I'll spit on it, I say. *I'll spit and spit until there's no fire left.*

I spit to demonstrate, and James laughs. I spit again. He spits. His laughter loud enough that I fear he'll wake the house.

Only once I tuck him into bed does he say, *Why are you holding a dress?*

It's a secret, I say, no longer worried. *It's a surprise for later.*

Okay.

When I go to my room. When I try on the dress, I—I—

No. I never try on the dress. I am too afraid of what I will see, too afraid of what I will not. It is like a diary or a dollhouse. Too permanent a thing.

But in that moment, I believe in Heaven and in Hell. I believe in souls without bodies. I believe the only way out of the dragon is to fight and to lose. Somewhere the sun is shining between new spring leaves. I don't know where I'll go after this. I hope that Patrick will be there. That there will be a crystal brook flowing between the trees. And he'll sit up, say, *Hey, space cadet, what took you so long?*

EVERY DISASTER MUST come on a day like any other. Ships sink and buildings fall and cliff-size waves crush homes, and somewhere there is *always* a shining sun. Somewhere there is a field, the shade of a century-old tree. Every day is the best of someone's life—even the day you die.

It is because I must die that I do it. I never wear the dress; I wrap myself in a cheap robe, stolen from my mother's closet.

I carve those crosses into the girls' skin. Selecting the pieces as I would doll parts. Chasing the beauty. It is that easy to become someone else. You don't have to sew a dress or a costume of girl flesh. You put yourself in the machine, in the belly of the dragon, and it does your dreaming for you.

I don't think of Heaven or Hell by the time I meet Beatrice in the basement. I don't think of the hours she came to my bed. I think only of the doll she broke seconds before. It had been a maiden—not quite a princess, because I am no longer a child. But a girl, certainly. High cheekbones and shallow brow. A blue robe fell across its knees. She smashed it into the floor. *Hey, fag-boy*, she said. *Come and do something about it, why don't you?*

Mr. Catten was wrong. Puppets may have their own life but so do the dolls. Anything you give attention is alive.

Naturally I wanted to take a life in return.

We circle each other in the basement. I find my knives easily. Weaponless Beatrice throws more dolls at me. I never fixed the wolf she broke that first night. Her blood stained the pillow.

You little bitch, Beatrice says. *You aren't going to stab me. You can't even get it up for me.*

I lunge, and she dodges and grinds another doll beneath her heel.

You were always such a goddamn freak. I knew you were some kind of faggot the first time I saw you. Still we circle, each waiting to die. *You know what they're going to do to you? They're going to lock you up in a tiny room with all the other faggots and each day they're going to zap the faggotry out of your brain. And at night all the other faggots are going to use your stupid little mouth. I'm probably the only person who's ever going to fuck you who doesn't have AIDS.*

You should kill yourself, she says, *because you don't have the guts to kill me.*

I lunge again, trip. Beatrice laughs.

You're pathetic, she says. *There's no world for people like you. There's nothing for you. At least in Hell you'll be with your own kind. At least when you're dead—*

There are no words left. No time to tell her that I agree and I long for it. That in death, some divine watchman will tell me whether I was saint or monster. That I will know at last how we all measure up.

There are no words. There is my knife in her eye, pushed back, back, back.

I am so tired. I want to sit and never rise. Let the dragon digest me at long last. There is no world left. No magic. Heaven and Hell are full of moldy tile. Heaven and Hell do not exist. There is blood on my robe, and a world three souls lighter.

I wonder how I will explain it to my twin. How I can get her to the hospital, get the knife out cleanly. Maybe we'll laugh about it after. Maybe things will be like they had been.

I am all smiles when she meets me with the knife. Of course, I think. At last. I do not let go of the railing at her first thrust. I hold on as long as I can, let her knife plunge in over and over. I fall back into the darkness with a look of bliss.

I can press myself to the wall and become house, then air, then sky. I'll watch the doll lives shuffle through its penciled walls. I'll see my parents with their arms entwined in love. See Calla and James in performing clothes. My sister in her darkroom with pictures of a beautiful world.

I will be wordless, nameless, and I will dance beautifully. I feel the late spring warmth and cool concrete. My crucifix has become a sword. My blood will hold up these walls. I will carry around my gouged-out eyes. Present my breasts on a silver platter, held by a puppet. And the woods will be full of the image of love. There will be real love at last.

And now—silence.

ACT II

THE NEXT YEAR

ONE

EDNA'S IN THE living room, alone again. Walkie-talkie in hand. Too anxious to pace.

She says: "What's happening?"

Wren's voice crackles through. "My room's clear!"

And James: "Upstairs linen closet is good to go, Eddie!"

Heather says, "The—uh, study is all clear."

"Wrennie, lock the door behind you."

"Already did, Mom."

"Calla?"

Calla sits in her bedroom, walkie-talkie propped beside her computer. The walls have been decorated with Francis Bacon and Cy Twombly prints. A silent box fan under the open window.

"I'm in the upstairs bathroom," she says. "No tranny slashers here."

"Okay," Edna says. "Okay."

That for-want feeling is loud. For want of a husband, a home, a kind and loving God. For want of a world without evil. If she could move, Edna would touch the face of the TV, the plywood over the windows. She'd touch the copies of Roger's book and the *Dollmaker* DVD. She would touch everything in the room once—the Chihuly paperweights and yellowing cross-stitch samplers and the postcards that Roger continues to send. Instead, she presses the walkie-talkie button, releases it without speaking. She chews her tongue. Five things she can see: the boards, the wedding photo she tore in half, the Scotch tape holding its pieces together. The empty shelves where there was once a record collection. The dark TV.

"Nothing in the piano room," James says. "Except a piano. And dust."

"Downstairs bathroom is empty. Should I check the basement, Mom?"

"No. Make your aunt or uncle do it. Where are you, Calla?"

"The attic," she says. She is still in her bedroom. The familiar clicking pauses. "God, it needs sweeping up here."

"That's—beside the point."

"Oh god, what is that?" Calla slams one hand against the desk and, briefly, scares herself.

"What?"

A pause. Calla stifles her laughter.

"Calla?"

"It must have been a rat. Looked about the size of a dachshund, though."

"Oh." Four things she can taste. No—it can't be taste. Feel? There is her threadbare cotton shirt. The walkie-talkie's plastic casing flexing in her hand. The floor almost tidal beneath her: advancing, receding in time with the night. Edna knows Calla's lying—and this scares her more than if she believed the lie. This family, with all its betrayals big and small.

"Attic is all set," Calla says.

"Good, please lock up."

"Cupboard under the stairs is clear!" Wren says.

"Ditto the guest room."

"Nothing in the sunroom."

"Okay, okay," Edna says. "Everyone lock up. The keys are in the doors." There is blood in her nail beds. She taps her foot to the rhythm of a half-remembered song. "Everyone?"

"Locked!"

"Everything's good, Mom!"

"Done and done!"

There is a too-long pause before Calla snatches up the walkie-talkie, which is when Edna knows for certain. "Yeah, all good!"

"Come down here then. I'll set the burglar alarm." Edna loosens. She riffles through Roger's postcards to prove that she can. And his letter—the ragged cheek of an opened envelope. "It's time to begin."

TWO

WREN, CALLA, HEATHER, and James cluster in the living room with their unlit candles. No one thinks to dim the lights.

"The night begins here," Edna says. "The night begins—oh, how does it start?"

"We need to light the candles," Wren says.

"Right."

Edna looks at one door out of the living room, then the other. Thumb between teeth. "Does anyone have matches?"

"I can get—"

"No, James, don't—"

"I have a lighter," Calla says. The flash of a silver Zippo, the flicked wheel and flickering flame. She lights her own candle and passes the flame from wick to wick.

"Okay," Edna says. "Where were we?"

"The night begins," Wren offers, and her mother picks up:

"The night begins. The St. Cloud parents are in Charlottesville. They're in Charlottesville with their tiny son and daughter, and they've left their older daughter all alone in the dark. Their older daughter and their—their sick—their son."

"Easy, Mom."

"There were Polly and Vera and there was Bea. There was Bea and there was me, all together in the dark. It's when the clock creeps into midnight that we decide to do the séance."

"It's by this burning," Wren says, "that they will make themselves known to the world of spirits."

It's almost a relief to see her mother so honestly at loose ends. To have a clear path toward helping. Co-narrating this night that gave them both life.

"We are meant to burn something of power. A photo, a pearl, a tooth. Only Bea thinks of something truly powerful. A body, made by a monster. The doll looks a little like her, in fact. The same bow mouth. The sweep of raven hair. It is as though by burning it, she will free a piece of her soul."

Wren says, "They close their eyes. Vera leads them in the séance. All the while, the family's older son—"

Edna: "Killer. Monster."

"—sneaks into the downstairs bathroom. He has hidden a knife behind the shower curtain. Laid it in the tub like an infant in her cradle."

Wren wonders what her forgotten uncle was really like. She asked her aunt, but Calla only snorted. *Your father literally wrote the book on it*, she said.

Before that, Wren insisted. *When he was young.*

He was always like that. The only miracle is that he didn't kill more people.

"It happens quickly," Wren says. "Polly goes to the bathroom and does not come back. The killer's knife goes through her throat, her heart. He will make her body, one of these bodies, his own."

Heather steps forward in perfect time. A brief pause; Wren gives her the customary tap on the heart, and Heather blows out her candle.

They do not move to the bathroom. Do not move to the front door. There they are, Heather thinks, all the odds and ends. How little changes in a year away. God—why had they come back? Why had James asked to marry her?

Edna says, "Bea thought we should hide. That it would be fun to scare Polly. At first I followed her into the basement, but she was making me giggle too much, putting the dolls in sexual positions. It's like some terrible dream, she said. It's like you're showing up to class with come stains on your dress. And I was hysterical, I had to hide alone."

"From her hiding place," Wren says, "Edna hears Vera's death. The knife across her throat, the gurgle of life leaving her. Symbols carved into flesh. A dream of thieving girlhood."

But why kill three? Or four, even? Wren's only answer: death is the St. Cloud birthright. She does not often think of her grandparents—she was too young to really know them. They were a stuffed bear at Christmas and those Gershwin songs. They were faces in faded photos. But they were proof that it was not only her uncle; anyone could kill or be killed. Death can be manufactured, sold for cash. This is why Calla calls their blood *cursed*. This is why Wren dreams of fire falling from the sky.

Two of Wren's fingers across her uncle's throat. Out goes James's candle.

"She calls out," Wren says.

"I call out," Edna says. "And he—stabbed me. That thing stabbed me."

"And before he can finish the job, she is saved by Bea."

"'Hey, fag-boy,' she said."

James: "Edna, I'm not sure—" But Heather hushes him.

"Bea throws a doll into the air," Wren says. "She strikes it with a hammer. It's beautiful, the way it smashes to pieces."

"And then they disappeared into the basement. We had just been down there," Edna says. "I kept thinking: If we had stayed together. If I hadn't been laughing. If I had loved her the right way."

Wren: "There is clatter and clamor, tools and dolls thrown this way and that. The police will find Bea with a knife in her eye."

Wren moves to touch Calla's eye. Calla is ready for it: lids shut, though she is smirking. A secret-keeper smile, shared between clandestine lovers across a crowded party.

Edna grabs her daughter's wrist. Says, "Please, don't."

No one moves. Calla's eyes flick open.

Wren says, "The ritual, Mom."

Another beat.

"Yes."

But Edna does not release her daughter's wrist. It is Edna, not Wren, who puts her fingers to Calla's lidded eye. Edna who blows out the candle. The room awaits her next move. I'm sorry, she thinks. She projects the thought backward in time. I'm sorry, I'm sorry. The words should have filled the house on that stray night in 1992. They should have been scratched into every bedpost. Written in ballpoint pen across her wrist, and Bea's, and Polly's, and Vera's. Like a reminder to study for a history test. Like a new friend's phone number. I'm sorry.

It isn't enough.

Wren does not resist when her mother takes the still-flickering candle from her. It is Edna's by right.

Edna says, "I never felt pain like when I pulled out the knife. It is the pain of a star dying. The pain of a worm splitting into two separate lives. When Roland arrives at the top of the stairs, I meet his heart with his own knife. It has my blood on it. Polly's. Vera's. Our deaths all mingling with his. Plunged down through the folds of that horrible dress. When I draw the blade out, I think of licking it clean—taking all this horror into myself—and turning the blade against myself. If he wants another body, well, here's one he can have. I will be free.

"But no. I plunge it again between his ribs. I throw him into the darkness. And in the darkness he remains."

THREE

THE DOORS ARE locked. Edna's candle burns in the kitchen through the sleepless night. And Calla sits again at her computer, back to the open window. She is—what else?—playing *The Neighborhood*. She has been living in this room a year now.

From the outer dark, a pale pair of hands inches the window open. Click, click. Calla does not notice. A figure in black, head hidden by a balaclava, steps into the room. It toes across the floor in stocking feet.

A hint of wind and jasmine. The shadow is behind Calla, hands reaching for her neck. Calla turns and—

"Boogity boogity!"

Calla leaps, hand already in a fist, but the shadow doubles over laughing.

"Goddammit, Sarah."

Calla peels the balaclava from the girl. Pale face and dark, dark hair.

"Had you, didn't I?" Sarah is bright and beautiful as a diamond from the mine. Sun-flashing and bloody.

"Keep your fucking voice down," Calla says, "or my sister will be in here with a gun."

"God, you sound like you're fifteen. 'Oh nooo, my *mommy* will find out!!' You're probably still scared of thunderstorms too."

"Shouldn't have told you about that." Calla's fist is still drawn back. She lowers it, kisses Sarah.

"Ah, no," Sarah says, quieter now. "That is a nicer use for this mouth."

Another kiss. Longer.

"Miss Fletcher, I believe it's a fortnight since I saw you last."

"Feels like a fortnight of fortnights," Sarah says. "A hundred and ninety-six nights without that kiss."

"Where are your shoes?"

"Right!"

Sarah reaches out the window, brings up a pair of combat boots and a six-pack of High Life.

Calla laughs. "How did you get that up the trellis?"

She clamps the cardboard handle between her teeth. "'ike thish!"

Sarah fumbles in Calla's pocket for the silver Zippo. It was a gift—*KINDLE MY HEART* scratched into its plain brown wrapping paper. She pops open a beer. Falls into the leather chair. Takes a swig.

"How was tour?" Calla asks.

"Normal." Another swig. "Weird. Wires crossed on the bill in Boston. Half the room was Nazi punks in baggy pants. A fight broke out in the parking lot after."

Calla laughs. "No, it didn't."

"There was a skinhead with BLUD and SOIL knuckle tatts. I literally had to break a bottle over his head. Clio and Frankie were, like, suplexing Jean Raspail fanboys left and right."

"Stop, stop." Calla's laughter is too much. It's such a bad idea to have Sarah here tonight. But a day without her touch, let alone two weeks, is a day spent drowning. Edna will never know.

"How's life in simulated suburbia?" Sarah asks.

"Why, you miss it?"

"I know you didn't get that vault open, or it would've been the first thing out of your mouth."

Calla says, "There've been more murders, actually."

"In the game, you mean."

"Right."

Five months ago, in the middle of the night, an in-game family of four was slaughtered. Bodies cut to pieces and strewn about the house. Written in blood across their windows and walls, again and again, one word: *FEVER*.

The same night, within maybe an hour, a nearly identical family was killed in western Ohio. Their children a perfect match for the scruffy blond moppets in *The Neighborhood*. The parents tall and good-looking. The houses didn't match but here, too, on the walls: *FEVER. FEVER. FEVER. FEVER.* No one in the family had ever played *The Neighborhood*. Their friends had never heard of it. They caught the kid who did it—a hollow-eyed nineteen-year-old whose avatar had skin like the night sky. Rumor was he'd become obsessed with the idea that the game was alive. He was being held in prison without bail.

No more real-life analogs, thankfully. Not yet. But there have been more murders in-game. The dismemberment, the *FEVER*.

This, Calla knows, is the difference between *The Neighborhood* and the useless plays she used to write. There's no curtain to fall, no props to reset for tomorrow's show. A play is bounded, safe. Real life isn't; the game isn't.

"You *know* the Tipper Gore crowd is eating this up," Sarah says. She hasn't played *The Neighborhood* since she and Calla met. "It's, like, gonna give them all the ammunition they need to get video games banned for good."

It's ridiculous to claim that video games *cause* violence. But they naturalize a rhetoric of violence. You become accustomed to it. The dead respawn, the burned-down houses come back. No one cany deny these things matter, now. The line between real and simulated is thinning.

"The last few deaths were the bloodiest yet," Calla says. "No one knows if it's an official patch or more proc-gen stuff or, like, some kind of pirate mod. Everyone who's here to play at suburban life is getting the worst of it." There's pressure, suddenly, to make your characters inhuman. To divorce the game bodies from those of the living. "They found a baby's head in the microwave."

"Fuck, they rendered that? Are there pics?"

"You're so demented."

"You love it. You're demented too." Another kiss. Sarah opens a second bottle, a third, hands one to Calla. They cheers.

Calla says, "You know what night it is, right?"

"Course, babes. I grew up in the literal shadow of your family home. I've seen the movie like everyone else."

"Only—checking." Impossible to imagine May 31 as a normal day. A day when you can talk about anything. Suplexing Nazis and new crimes.

"Is that what you were thinking about?" Sarah asks. "When you saw me coming up behind you?"

"I wasn't thinking anything. It's an ordinary human fear—a stranger in your room."

"You didn't think I was that killer tranny brother of yours? Hopping in for a bit to see if you could cut my dick off?" Sarah could be talking weather. No narrowed eyes, no grimace. Only the bottle to her lips. A glance toward the open night.

"That's Edna's worry," Calla says, "not mine."

"You think I have tranny proportions? You think my wrists and shoulders are too big?"

"You know I don't."

"Like I'm playing at being a woman?"

"Sarah—"

Sarah pulls a gun from her waistband. She does not aim it at Calla or herself but still—it's a fucking gun.

"Is that what you think I look like? Yes or no, Callie."

"Jesus fucking Christ—"

"Answer the question." And still that calm.

"No! Obviously not!"

Sarah smiles. She spins the gun around her finger. Calla, for all her years in theater, cannot tell if it's real or a prop.

"I'm only joking, babes."

Calla sets down her beer so that Sarah will not see her hands shake. "Usually jokes have punch lines."

"Well, how's this."

The gun vanishes. Sarah stands, presses her lips to Calla's. A hand on her cheek. A hand slipping past the waistline of her shorts.

"That'll—do nicely." At the first touch, Calla can barely breathe. It's new again every time. The tension of Sarah's fingers teasing her open. The relief when her fingers find Calla's clit—and Calla breathes more deeply than she ever has.

They fall into bed. More kissing, more hands. Calla bucks toward Sarah's touch but distractedly—one ear on the hallway, the stairs.

"Hey," Sarah says with that diamond smile. "Where are you?"

"Sorry, it's . . ."

"I know, I know." Her touch gentler now. "You ever have dates sneak back here in high school?"

Never mind that this wasn't Calla's childhood room. Never mind that the St. Cloud parents never monitored her behavior. The worst had already happened; what did it matter if she got pregnant, or shot heroin, or cut herself?

"Not really."

"Well, what if we pretend?" An easy rhythm: Sarah's hands, her words, Calla's breath. "You're the beautiful cheerleader, home after the big game. I'm the gothy punk girl no one sits with at lunch. But you still see me, standing at the hurricane fence by the football field. You see my fingers linked through the wire, my eyes watching you as you jump up and down. And you think about how nice those fingers look. How they'd feel inside you."

Calla gasps as Sarah, finally, works one finger, then a second, inside her.

Sarah goes on: "And I follow you home. And I climb up the trellis. And you don't ask what I'm doing here. You don't need to tell me that your mom will kill you if she finds me. We meet like two notes in the same chord, tolling out across the land. And it's perfect. It's good."

FOUR

WREN, DRESSED IN her mother's old overalls, stands against the wall of her mother's room. James is cross-legged on the floor, with Edna standing over him. She reads Roger's letter as though reading a poem to a child.

"*And the second question,*" she reads, "*no less difficult than the first, is: How to end? How do things wrap up? In life, we are tempted to call an act final. The curtain falls on what we have had—our old house, job, love—and we pretend we will never come to it again. The truth is that we return over and over. We see the walls of those old rooms in dreams. We come together as lovers in a hundred memories.*"

All James can think to say is, "Oh, jeez."

"Wait, it gets worse." Wren will perhaps always be mad at her father for leaving. But she, too, feels the threads that hold her loosening.

"*The curious thing about being a writer is that you must dwell in the recesses of memory that others relinquish. The littlest moments. A tryst, which means no more than a passing storm to the other party, becomes the basis for a book—the work of years. A note passed in the back of a school bus becomes ten thousand words of character development.*

"*You may remember, dear doe, that before I was a historian of horrors, I had hoped to be a novelist. I was never good at holding on to these things.*

I hated to return to the pains I bore and bored into others. The night, say, I smashed my mother's crystal fruit bowl—the only beautiful thing she owned. Instead, I worked my way into other lives. I could descend on them for a brief moment—a year, say—and etch their image onto the page."

"And, what," James says, "that's you?"

"That's the implication, isn't it?" Wren says. She shifts her weight and her shoulders dig into the wall. Her mind isn't on her father, or her mother, or the evening's push-pull candle fantasy. She thinks only of *The Neighborhood.*

Edna massages the old scar below her collarbone. Her arm is unseasonably sore, as though a cold front were moving in. "*But of course I couldn't leave you,*" she goes on. "*Who could leave the bright, quick-witted girl who loved Ernst Lubitsch and Diane Arbus? You already proved, in loving me, that it is impossible to leave anything behind.*"

James listens, expectant.

"*Love, Roger.*"

"And you consider this *good* news?"

"Oh, you didn't listen, Jamie. Read it for yourself." She thrusts the letter to him and he scans it. "There at the end, don't you see? *It's impossible to leave anything behind.*"

". . . right."

"He still loves me. As I've always maintained. As you and your sister have worked so hard to disabuse me of."

James says, "Would you want him to come back? Would you really?"

"As far as I'm concerned," Wren says, "he can fucking rot in California like an overripe orange."

"Language, Wrennie."

Wren can't understand why he hasn't come back. It is one thing to zip back and forth across the country and sleep with a woman closer to Wren's age than her mother's. But to go there and to stay. To abandon the hermetic golden world they made together. It's one more blow from the St. Cloud blood. By crook or by sword they will push, push, push.

Not that the family needs as much care as her father thinks. Edna has been photographing Wren. Wren has been reading, playing the game, studying for the GED. She phones Roger regularly. Perhaps *abandoned* isn't the word; Wren feels ancillary to the whole thing.

Edna says, "I know you think you understand, Jamie, but the bond of marriage is unique. It's a choice you make and go on making. You have to be willing to forgive each other a lot." She holds out a hand and he takes it, hauls himself up. She does not let go once he's standing. "When are you and Heather getting married?"

"Oh." He'd been pretending, more or less, that Heather had said *yes*; she hadn't said *no*. It was a weird time—the boys, the skirt—but if you can't ask someone to marry you at a weird time, what good is asking at a normal one? "We're getting around to it."

"If it's a matter of money—"

"No, no."

Edna shakes the letter emphatically. "Let this be your encouragement. Marriage is a tie between you and the other, a tie that transcends death. It's bigger than the grasping, money-grubbing embrace of some shallow whore."

Wren says, "Language, Edna."

"We'll keep that in mind, Eddie. That's, uhm, very helpful." James opens the door to leave.

"Off to watch your movie?" Edna asks.

"Yeah, maybe." He goes, leaving the door open. Edna counts to five and crosses the room. Shuts and locks it.

"You might as well not do that," Wren says. "I'm headed to my own room soon."

"Are you going to leave me too, Wren?"

What would be perfect, Wren thinks, is if her mother were a kind of eldritch hermit crab. If she could wander across the land, carrying the house on her back, only poking her head out now and then to get a whiff of cut grass and gasoline.

"I'll be downstairs, Mom. You can come read with me, if you want."

A silence.

"Sometimes," Edna says, "I wonder what the point of surviving that night was."

"Oh, Mom, don't."

"Let me finish, Wren. Sometimes I look at what's left of my life. A big house that's emptier all the time."

"No, we traded Dad for Calla."

"I look at photos that mark, if anything, the decline in one woman's talent. I see a legacy of books and films and outrage and fear that would go on just the same without me. But I look at you, Wren, and I think: Thank God. Thank God I lived long enough to see such a wonderful daughter into the world. And if I go on living, it's so I can make that world safer for you. Raise up this little ritual like a prayer, to protect you and your father and your aunt and uncle. But don't leave me, Wren. Don't. If that makes you mad—furious—I'll take your anger, be your whipping boy, whatever. I'll take it the rest of my life if it keeps you safe."

The single candle in the kitchen. Burning a hole in the night.

"I'll be fine," Wren says.

"Tell me. Tell me you'll come back to this house. No matter how far life takes you, to whatever foreign shores. On this night, each year, for as long as we both live. Promise you'll be here."

"I'll be here, Mom."

"That's a good girl."

FIVE

SARAH DOZES, NAKED but for the sheets wrapped around her. Calla is already at the computer. She's lost interest in the vault lately, hasn't burned down the Spitehouse in months.

It's a miracle the game brought Sarah to her. *I know this house btw*, she'd said. Calla would've believed no prediction of love. She'd have spat in the face of any oracle. Yet here it was: a life worth having.

This is her second experience with a woman. But fingerfucking her freshman roommate was categorically different. That girl gasped emptily, asked to cuddle. No different from sex with men. For years Calla had stumbled up their stairs after some cast party, some ecstatic Lupercalia, and taken cold pleasure in the things she could do to their bodies. She didn't go on dates if she could help it—only found her way to their beds and made them call her name, erupt in pleasure, and pass out. She got herself off in bed beside them, drowning out their sleeping breath.

People did fall in love with her. That was how she knew it was time to leave them.

But Sarah. It's as though a handful of red threads stretch between Calla's chest and Sarah's hands. Like the lacing on some exotic garment. Sarah pulls, and everything in Calla tightens.

Most bewildering: Sarah isn't scared of who she is. She knows and isn't scared.

After the movies started coming out, Calla told one of those boys back in college, *you could get the mask at any Halloween shop in the country. Picture me, at the bedroom window, watching a horde of them tromp to the door. Pasty face and clownish slap of lipstick. I think half of them didn't know what house it was. And there are two competing truths in your head at that moment. The first is obvious: that isn't him. It isn't even a representation of him, it's an echo of an echo. That actor, who played him in the movie, which came out of the book, which came out of life.*

The second is: of course that's him. There's a piece of him in every stupid rubber face. And a piece of him in hers. *The man, the monster, the legend. Everyone remembers how he killed the girls. The moment they hear my name—what else could they think of?*

Sarah stirs. "How long was I out for?"

"Not long. Forty minutes."

"Come back to bed?" she says. Calla keeps clicking. "Please?"

Calla quits, flops into the bed, and kisses Sarah. Sarah digs through the pile of clothes for a cigarette. Calla widens the window, sets the box fan blowing outward. The silver Zippo and her lover's cigarette. For an ashtray, a red Solo cup with a crust of grape soda. The bedside table sits at an angle to the wall, knocked in their furtive fracas. Calla throws the lighter there. Let it all be a glorious disarray.

"How can you play that game," Sarah asks, "when you have such a beautiful girl in your bed?"

"How can you sleep when you're in such a beautiful girl's room?"

Sarah sucks her Newport, blows into the fan.

"What were you up to? More vault shit?"

"There was a gathering at the latest murder scene," Calla says. "So many people in attendance they could barely render; the whole thing was lagging."

"Where'd this one happen?"

"This house on the edge of a bottomless canyon. There's a stream that falls into the abyss and disappears. The house is modern. Mostly glass. Only wall enough to hide the bedroom and bath."

"Inviting break-ins."

"Anyway, there's still blood on the walls. These bright-red splashes."

"If it were real blood," Sarah says, "it'd turn brown."

"It is real, though. Somehow it is. These hundreds of avatars turning up to see the site of a digital slaughter. The fear that this is going to be the next one to leak into the real world. Whoever's avatars got killed, they remade the whole family from scratch. Two fathers, two daughters."

Since the Fever murders started, none of the dismembered avatars respawned. Their souls had blinked out of existence and never blinked back. Some people took this as a sign to stop playing forever, or to start over. But others desperately recrafted the slain. Trying to remember their exact hair color, the width of their nose, the arch of their eyebrows. Calla thinks it's the most fearful thing they can do—bringing back the dead.

Maybe the religions that banned representational art were onto something. There is so much power in an image of the world.

Calla goes on: "The four of them were standing there, inside the house, looking out through the blood at the juddering bodies. And you know that somewhere, in some corner of the world, there's a real person looking through the window of their computer. They're a spectacle now. The death is real and it isn't. The fear. These things leak through."

"Yeah, but it's just a bunch of people sitting alone," Sarah says. "Watching shadows on the wall of a cave and pretending that's life."

"Bold words from a girl who fell in love sitting alone."

"Yeah, yeah. I played for, like, three weeks."

"*And* you watch every goddamn episode of *The Bachelor*." Sarah wouldn't make plans on Monday nights for fear of missing an episode. "Talk about shadows on a cave wall."

"Okay, that *isn't* the same at all. Those people are literally in love." Sarah had justified herself many times: The show's magic was that everything happened in reverse. There is an image of love—dates in exotic locales, the single-minded focus on romance—and love follows.

And in *The Neighborhood*: lives made, lives taken. An image of death becomes death itself.

Calla says, "People did die."

"One time. Everything since then is fake. You only feel differently because you're a theater kid at heart." And it's true that Sarah wasn't going to fuck Calla in the game. Wasn't going to tighten all those strings.

But Calla can't let it go. "Sorry we can't all live that punk lifestyle, Sare-bear. Some of us are afraid to die."

"Sure." A beat, a breath. More smoke in the night. "Have you thought any more about what we talked about?"

"Not tonight, Sarah."

"Tonight more than ever!"

"I—can't think about it," Calla says. "It's like you're asking me to scale a brick wall with my bare hands."

"We could have it so good. We could host all our friends for weeks. Play lawn darts in the summer. Dine on catfish and champagne every goddamn night. We could fill this house with art."

"Not *this* house." Calla shouldn't even say the words. The fear of making it happen by naming it. "Not if we burn it down."

"You know what I mean. What good is it doing your sister?" It's the place they grew up. The place they all return to. But it is Edna's—Edna's alone. And it'll be Wren's, and then her children's—and then and then and then. "It's evil," Sarah says, "her having all this money. Knowing where it came from. It's fucking blood money. Your mom and dad knew it. It made them sick."

"Right. Enough."

"I'm only saying, babes. Imagine the life we could make for ourselves if we had that money. We could start a record label. A studio in the basement. A garden full of the sweetest tomatoes you've ever tasted."

"Who eats tomatoes for their sweetness?"

Sarah goes on: "A van to take us around the country. We'll camp in the foothills. We'll make a sky of new constellations. A life we deserve. You deserve. What were the odds of us finding each other, huh?" Sarah runs her hands over Calla's, up her arms. That electric touch. "You know how many people meet the actual goddamn love of their life in a game like that? No one, babes, fucking no one. And I knew—the first time I ever saw you burn it down, I knew. That's how our love will burn. That's how we'll make our new world together. A forest burning for new growth. The haunted house of my childhood and yours—gone for good."

Sarah relished telling Calla the child-myths of the St. Cloud home. The halls' host of translucent figures. The murders multiplied. Girls came out of its darkened doorways—they did, she swears they did—with their tits cut off and one eye gouged out. Drunk on peach schnapps, Sarah's friends dared each other all the way to the door, and scattered when the bell rang through this hollow place.

Calla was gone by then. She was gone, and Sarah was a child.

"It was fate we met," Sarah says. "What comes next is fate too."

"Sarah—"

"Burn down this house with me."

"It's not like Edna would split the insur—"

"One step at a time, babes. This place is hurting you. We wipe that away, we have a future."

What else can Calla say? How does anyone once loveless refuse the demands of love?

"Okay," she says. "Yes."

Sarah grabs her face in both hands, kisses her. The cigarette burns inches from Calla's ear. "Oh, baby, you're going to love what comes next." Sarah dashes the cigarette dark, scrambles to the mattress's edge, shuffles into her clothes.

Calla laughs. "Where the Hell are you going?"

"To get champagne! The future starts tonight."

Sarah pulls the fan from the window.

"Sarah, stay—"

There's a knock at the door. Both women freeze.

"Calla?" James's voice. Get under the bed, Calla thinks. Fucking hide Sarah do you have any idea—but the door swings open. Sarah in the middle of the room in her black jeans and bra. James holds a chocolate cupcake with a single candle in it. Everyone is the deer; everyone is the headlights.

"Hi," he says. "I'm James."

"Sarah. Charmed." She salutes Calla. "See you in a bit, babes." Rumpled shirt in one hand and boots in the other, she scarpers out the window and into the night. Leaving half a six-pack, cigarette smoke, her sweat on Calla's tongue.

"She seems nice," James says.

"It's not what you think."

"She isn't nice?"

Calla sighs, falls back into bed. "Why are you holding a cupcake?"

"Oh!" He spies the lighter. Calla ashamed of the disordered table, the ashtray cup. When the candle is lit: "Happy returniversary!"

A beat.

"You've been back for a year," he says.

"Even I'm too superstitious to blow out a candle tonight."

"Oh. Fuck."

"Leave it on the table. We'll put it outside in the morning."

He straightens the table, tips some wax onto it, fixes the cakey candle-end between lighter and cup. Like an altar to a child's abandoned birthday party.

"So what is it?" James asks.

"You're the one who came in here."

"I mean, if it's not what it looks like, with the girl—what is it?"

Calla bites her lip, her tongue, her cheek. Each gentle stab a reminder of her lover's missing touch. For all her adulthood, Bringing Someone Home was impossibly formal, a capitalized offense. Exposing her choices to scrutiny. It would be so much easier, wouldn't it, to have a string of loveless affairs and be perpetually unknowable and die at some chic age like forty-five. Your grave attended by handsome, stupid men carrying identical Eddie Bauer umbrellas. Then you'd never have to define yourself. You'd just be you, in perpetuity.

"It's a thing that's happening," she says.

"Are you gay now?"

"You're twenty-six, Jamie. I shouldn't have to tell you that bisexuality exists."

James can't hide his conspiratorial pleasure. "I've had some experience myself," he says. "With men, I mean."

"No, you haven't, you little liar." None of them were—none of them could have been—"When?"

"This last year. Heather and I opened things up."

"You little scamp! How is it?" Calla sitting up now—bright-eyed, thrilled. James hadn't planned on telling her; maybe it was a mistake. No one back upstate ever asked a question like this. Heather's friends confessed they'd always assumed he was some flavor of queer.

But how *was* it? There were like a hundred codes and shibboleths that he didn't know. There were men who wanted more than he could give. And there were moments that felt like a long-sought truth. His face shoved into the drywall or bed frame as his date for the night entered him, squeezing past that ring of initial resistance, filling him up, up, up. Moments when a sealed door cracked open, and he thought he'd never want more than this.

He rarely got hard during these encounters. Some men didn't care—happy to use his ass and mouth and clean themselves off, kick the raw wound of him back into the world. Some tried for an hour to coax him erect. Begging for him to fill them up. Begging for his come. He left these hookups feeling like he'd bombed a job interview.

"It's—I mean, it's okay," he says.

Calla smirks. "Maybe you're doing it for attention."

"Well, if I am, it's not working much. Are you going to eat that cupcake? Because Heather made it and—"

"Help yourself, faggot."

"I don't think you're allowed to say that, even if you are gay." The cake is rich and moist and delicate. James takes tiny bites, savoring it. On the table, the candle burns too quickly. It will obviously not last the night. "Don't get me wrong," he says, "the sex is good. But, I dunno, it's not what I want." Another bite of cupcake. If Heather left him, he would never eat cake again. Each delicious bite would remind him only of his loss.

He says, "Heather likes to watch sometimes."

Calla, with her own diamond smile: "I need you to repeat that."

"To watch me, uhm. Get fucked." Heather never outright insists, which is maybe what saves it from being weird. Sitting in the corner, watching some cuddly, sweaty guy fill James's ass. Heather's hand in her shorts. She never insists, but she asks him to name the feeling. To describe it—his body stretching to hold them. The clarion ache of his prostate. He doesn't want to talk to Calla about this but who else is there? Not Manny, not Gretchen, not any of the friends he's appropriated from Heather.

Calla says, "I never pegged Heather—sorry, poor word choice—for such a freak."

"Can we talk about literally anything else?" The problem is that Heather loves it so much. If her stifled moans are anything to go by, she enjoys it more than he does. "What's your girlfriend's name?"

"Sarah. She told you."

"I wanted to see your face when you said it." It's charming to see Calla in love. The first, uncomplicated blush of it all. He never thought this day would come. "What's her story?"

"She plays in a punk band called Whileaway. She smokes Newports. She can fit her whole fist inside me."

"Sounds like a gem."

"She is. I don't really understand it."

James finishes the cupcake and wishes he had another. These evenings used to be so simple. "What's to understand?" he asks.

"How it happened. What the point is."

"Presumably it makes you happy."

"Sure, but what next? I keep living in this nowhere place? Fuck my girlfriend in our childhood playroom? I don't want to keep feeling like a kid." At least when she was a writer, there was a sense of progress. The steady rhythm of revision and rehearsal. Opening night. It may have been a lie, a distraction from the real. But who doesn't love a good distraction?

"Why don't you come stay with me and Heather in Kingston? You can bring Sarah."

"Oh, great, and then I can hear you getting bummed by beefcakes through the walls."

"Some people would pay a lot for that privilege."

"Perverts, James. Call them what they are."

A silence.

"What keeps you going?" Calla asks. "Apart from the anal sex, I mean."

"Okay, I officially regret telling you—"

"Joking, joking. Settle the fuck down."

"I don't know that anything keeps me going," James says. "Is that how you think about life? I guess the assumption is that one day I'll get over how we are. All of us. I'll figure out precisely what our damage is and free myself—float away. Like a kite with a miles-long tail."

Their childhood was free of the usual dramas—yelling parents and starvation wages. The great and terrible thing that altered the course of their lives came on a night they were out of town. A gap at the center. A black hole that makes the galaxy spin.

Calla only says, "Do you think this is how Roland felt?"

"Eddie doesn't like us to say his name."

"Can't say anything with you," she mutters.

"I have no idea how he felt. I assume everyone who takes drastic action feels like it's the only option."

"Like opening up their relationship?"

He ignores her. "They're probably right, is the thing. Like, you can wait for the world to go on turning. Wait for the feeling to fade. But I think sometimes, you don't have the tools for the job. That's a stone you can't roll away, an unfillable pit. And sometimes you can decide to live with that. And sometimes you can't. You can let it kill you or you can do something else about the pain."

Not the answer she'd hoped for. "Inspiring," she says.

"Look at our family, Calla. It's a miracle we aren't all shooting each other in the face."

SIX

THERE'S A COPY of *To the Lighthouse* beside Wren on her bed, a bookmark stuck at the two-thirds mark. It's been there for weeks. Wren is on her laptop, clicking like her aunt.

She's beginning to think the vault isn't a door at all. She had a dream last night that it swung open, revealing an impossibly deep blackness beneath. The house pitched forward, shrank to a point. Everything striated and turning, turning, turning. The walls went down, and the ceiling. The trees and the grass and the blue of the sky. In the end, there was nothing but darkness—a trillion miles in every direction.

Whoa, MiekeShaw types. *That sounds pretty heavy.*

It was and it wasn't, writes Wren. Her little bucket golem stands beside the avatar of a perfectly normal girl. *Is it clichéd if I say there was real peace there?*

MiekeShaw: *I have no idea.*

MiekeShaw: *Doesn't sound clichéd to me!*

Wren's golem tries the vault handle. Locked, unyielding as always. She's tried an adamantine pickaxe, a dragon-tooth-tipped crossbow bolt, every random key she can find. With the volume all the way up, it sounds like the vault is breathing.

A game like *Adventure* is limited—a database of a few options. It's like reading a book. If something breathes there, it's a hint of how to play, how to move on. Here, it may signify nothing at all. *The Neighborhood* is an organism—all possibility and randomness.

MiekeShaw: *Did you hear about the latest murders?*

Am I awful if I say I don't really care?

MiekeShaw: *No :) I don't really care either*

MiekeShaw: *It must be spooky, though. To have your avatar die.*

There's pressure, now, on people like Mieke to make their avatars look less human. The game grows distant from real life—extrapolates into alien territory. Impossible houses, bodies, art. Maybe soon it will break apart, Wren thinks. The trees and the grass and the error-screen sky.

Games—all games—*do something* to you, Wren thinks. You play to figure out what.

She and Mieke exchanged numbers a week ago, but neither has called the other yet. Anyone could be anyone once you leave *The Neighborhood*. Wren believes Mieke is who she claims to be: nineteen, a Rutgers student, interested in Japanese history. Sometimes they sit in the basement of Calla's digital house just to chat. Mieke got Wren to watch the first season of *Sherlock*, although Wren insisted that, quote, *Anything based on the work of a man who believed in the Cottingley Fairies was probably not worth my time*. (Goddamn was Martin Freeman sexy, though.) Wren told her about Dostoevsky and Wharton and Melville. (*People say the stuff about whales and the color white is boring, but those were my favorite parts!*) Mieke told her about seventeenth-century Japanese laws forbidding the use of firearms. (*Suddenly everyone had to go back to using swords*, she said, *under penalty of death*.)

Wren talks in vague terms about the stuff she's researched—St. Cloud Petrochem, gelled gasoline, the fires that burned away the old world and left the new one wretched, fresh, and stinging pink.

Mieke knows all about the firebombing of Tokyo. *Do you think money might be evil?* Wren asked. She's never mentioned her family by name. *Not only if it comes from an evil place, but the money itself?* She's been reading about chattel slavery, the cotton money that made America rich, which in turn financed so many wars. About the United Fruit Company destabilizing Central America, in turn creating the migrant crisis. And about her own family—the deaths that made their fortune. The curse of it all.

Because it is a curse. It must be. During her clandestine phone calls with Roger, she asks about her grandparents, her uncle, the early days of her parents' romance. And in return he says: *The only way out is out. The only way to win is not to play.* He gets cryptic when he drinks.

Was there a way out? Was it possible to turn a few months of cute animal pics and TV recommendations into a flesh-and-blood friendship?

Mieke writes, *What are you reading right now :)* and Wren struggles to respond. There are all these assumptions underlying Mieke's questions: an ordinary girl from an ordinary family, nothing worse than homework hanging over Wren. She'll go to college, she'll be an English major. (*You'll probably work at the writing center,* Mieke said, *wherever you go. They're the BEST.*) Is this how life works? Can you just leave home? It hadn't worked that way for her mother. It hadn't worked that way for anyone. Only her dad—the lone other Merrilow—was remotely free.

A knock at the door returns Wren to her room. She mutes the computer, says, "It's open!" Heather comes in. "How's the basement looking?"

"It's good," Heather says. Wren can't see why her mom asked Heather, of all people, to check. Opening-night jitters? Missing Roger, maybe? Missing her own parents. When Grandma and Grandpa were alive, it was like a protective spell. There hadn't yet been this pattern of catastrophe. Heather hovers, asks, "I was wondering if you've seen James around?"

"He was in my mom's room a little while ago."

"Ah yeah, that's probably it."

Wren sends Mieke a message laden with caveats. Explains that she's slowly getting through Woolf. She can't examine the vault that often, only when Calla's avatar isn't home. But the rest of the time, she's thinking about it. Hypothesizing how to free whatever it holds.

"What're you up to here?" Heather asks.

"This, mostly." Wren beckons her to watch. The bucket golem sprays liquid nitrogen into the vault's lock. Takes a hammer to it. Nothing.

"You can really do anything in there, huh?"

"That's the idea," Wren says. Mieke abruptly goodbyes, logs out. She does this. But—was Wren boring her? Was she too gruff about the murders? Is there some alchemical mix of wit and anecdote that would have gotten her to stay? "Some people are really freaked out by that degree of freedom. Like, they think it gives credence to the idea that we're all living in a simulation."

"How do they figure?"

"Oh, the obvious ways. If there are fewer limitations on what the digital can be, it gets harder to distinguish between it and our world. And then there are people who think that this is the grand, cyber-utopian turning point. That soon we're going to live in a digital space of endless possibility. Bodies won't be bodies in any meaningful way, just sacks of meat suspended in Herman Miller chairs."

Heather asks, "So which camp do you fall into?"

"Mostly I really want to get this door open." It's fun to explain the game to someone. She doesn't tell her mother for fear of having her privileges limited. *You never know who those people are,* she'd say. *You told them your NAME?* But to show off the game, where every move has meaning only as a move—it's like dancing. Or what Wren (never one of those leotard-ballet-jazz-tap girls, the girls who tore pages from her books and called her fat) assumes dancing is like.

Heather watches Wren's golem circle the vault.

"Uh," Wren says. "How are things with you and Uncle James?"

"Why?"

"You're hovering."

"Oh. Sorry." Heather steps back. But to leave now would be to admit something was wrong. "It's this night, you know? It's so skin-crawling."

"I don't know," Wren says. "I'm used to it."

"You don't really mean that, do you? I don't see how anyone could get used to this."

"The scary stuff has always been outside. I've never quite learned what I'm supposed to be afraid of." Wren can feel herself lightly lying, cosseting this woman who's half again her age. Treating Heather, outsider that she is, like a child. Wren *had been* used to it. For years this night was like some inverted Halloween. Instead of roaming the streets, hiding your flame in a pumpkin's grin—you retreat, you lock down. You burn your flames in the open. But now—what is it now?

"Let me ask you something," Wren says. "Does James ever talk about St. Cloud Petrochem?"

"I'm sorry?"

"About the fire." Wren cannot bring herself to name the cities—Dresden, Tokyo, Saigon. "The family legacy."

"All that stuff got sold a long time ago, didn't it? It's not like any of you are profiting from it now."

"Yeah," Wren says. "I guess." In all the hours she's spent googling the family, the most shocking discovery is that Calla did not tell a single lie. The weapons contracts and manufacture. The divestment. Even the fucking Appalachian folk songs. Her mother must not think about it. How could you go on living here if you did?

And there are harder questions—ones she no longer wants to ask Heather. Her mother was only a year older than Wren when the murders happened. When she met Wren's father.

"I don't think Jamie is used to it," Heather says at last. "This night."

"Why do you say that?"

"Little things. Biting his nails, chewing his cheeks. He's been taking out all these movies from work. Not only *Dollmaker*, but *The Crying Game* and *Dressed to Kill* and *Summer Loving*. There's this weird way it feels like he's preparing." Heather feels far from her teenage bedroom. The posters for Jimmy Eat World and *Jawbreaker*. The encyclopedia set she inherited from her grandmother. She used to look at the inset maps: the names of countries that didn't exist any longer, the borders redrawn. The world could just—change.

Heather isn't going to let James fuck things up. Their life is so much better now. Like anything that catches you by surprise, it is impossible to imagine letting go of the boys. Her chair in the corner. Coming so hard she thought she'd pass out. Give that up? Get married? Jesus Christ.

She says, "It gets to him, that's all. I know he dreams about what would be possible if he were from a normal family. Unhaunted by the stories and the movies, the killing and the dying."

What killing, Wren thinks, what dying could she mean? The Technicolor deaths he forces himself to watch on repeat? The version of Roland her father wrote about? What were these three little deaths versus the millions that were the family legacy?

"You guys really make adulthood seem dismal," Wren says.

And Heather laughs. What else could she do? "It isn't, really. It's only that you carry around so much inside you. The weight of who you used to be and who you'll still become." She looks to where Wren's avatar waits. A gently bobbing creature without eyes, mouth, heart. "Hence *The Neighborhood*, I guess. The chance to toss it all aside."

"Ah," says Wren. "She's a utopian."

"Am I?" Heather laughs again, a little less sure. "Well, why not? Someone in this house ought to be."

SEVEN

SEVEN YEARS OF nail holes dot the living room molding. Plywood mounted over window glass for one night, peeled off in dawn's safety. If they'd planned ahead, Edna thinks, they would have installed some kind of bracket. Wood easily fixed and unfixed, hardware hidden by the sweep of curtains. But she'd find a permanent fixture untrustworthy. She wants no space between board and wall. To feel the nails sink into the wood and hold fast. It's the same reason she doesn't like the burglar alarm. Only material can protect them.

For want of a nail. For want of a thicker board, a bulletproof window. Every house is a mess of openings. One day, she thinks, every St. Cloud will be dead. We will be dead and the house will be here. There will be mosses in the living room. Squirrels under the floorboards. The house will be eaten through as if by a cancer, and still it will not crumble.

She's never boarded up the bedroom windows before, but she needs something to fill tonight. She measured, bought extra plywood. The sound of her hammer rings through the house and does not bear remarking on for a single member of the St. Cloud clan.

Edna likes the uncertainty over whether it's dark outside or day. Even if it's a contrivance: the moment the night is over, she feels it. The lightness. To have survived again. To have survived.

The fortifications take all of thirty minutes. There is lots of night left to kill, and so she goes to the darkened living room and takes the DVD from the shelf. A cheap case, three commentary tracks. Roger did one of them. He'd thought it might lead to other jobs—talking heads in true-crime documentaries. More Hollywood work never manifested. Maybe that's why—maybe—maybe—

She really believed he'd come back for tonight. After all, he's *going* to come back—why not now? On this night that gave them everything. This night, made all the more famous by their love. The sanctity and security of the unit was their greatest strength—so, how could he still be in California? No one has ever died in California.

She takes the DVD to her bedroom, her fortress within the fortress. Sometimes she catches a whiff of her mother's perfume, the Johnson & Johnson baby powder she dusted her feet with. And then it's gone like a dream.

EDNA DOESN'T REMEMBER much of the premiere. The black Dolce & Gabbana dress, the soft hands of the woman doing her makeup. The fabled red carpet was thin and cheap under her black ballet flats. Dressed for a funeral, she'd later think.

She was six months pregnant; Wren was like a frog, a fish, turning over inside her. *Will it hurt her?* she asked. *If the movie's too scary, will it traumatize—* The makeup artist laughed. *Honey, I smoked through three pregnancies and my boys are fine.*

The film begins. There are high school scenes shot on that harmless coast. There are plaid dresses and baggy jeans. So slowly does it build. A gentle turning of the screw. At the premiere, she closed her eyes and held Roger's hand. Her other hand resting on her belly. She knew then, she's always known, that the film would replace her memories. One day her mind would reach for an image of Bea in her red leather jacket and find only an actress—a face that's gone on to crime shows and medical dramas. Not her friend, just an idea.

Maybe the movie had softened her. Maybe she hoped to be more like the docile girl-hero whom audiences let themselves love. Or maybe she had always been that way; the character must have come from somewhere.

When Bea's actress spoke, Edna broke out in goose bumps. She only opened her eyes to look at the crowd of faces. The wonder in their eyes, the spell of it all. The actor—taller than her twin brother—zipping himself into a too-tight dress while Shirley Bassey plays: *I can only watch you . . .*

At the after-party there'd been chandeliers and champagne light. People congratulated her on the film as though she'd done more than not die. She spent most of the party sitting by a piano while a man her father's age played jazz standards. Bea's actress came over with a crystal tumbler.

Don't worry, it's just club soda, she said.

They drank and watched the crowd. Edna could not tell if she felt choked because this woman was famous or because she was so beautiful.

How far along are you? the actress asked.

Thirty weeks.

Ahh, December baby. You'll have to make her birthday special.

We will. Edna could not wait to lie down. To rub oil over her swollen belly. To watch some stupid sitcom on the hotel TV. *There won't be a single day she doesn't know we're grateful for her.*

You must be ready for it.

I am, Edna said. Then: *What do you mean?*

Having a kid as young as we are. It's brave. You're really committing.

Committing—like a bit, a crime, a suicide. Of course Edna wanted a child. From the moment she first heard that beating heart, she swore her life would be different. No more hostility, no more rage. Only protection, and goodness, and love.

They're the future, Edna said. *And so on.*

That they are. The actress waved to a passing tuxedo, a Gucci gown. *I never like these things*, she said. *No one is honest with you. What are you celebrating, except that something's finished?*

Maybe finishing is enough.

The actress shook her head. *Maybe.*

You were *really great, though. You were exactly like her.* Edna hadn't meant to come out and say it. But there was the light, the music, the flashbulb diamonds still sparkling in her eyes.

Thanks.

I mean it. There was blood in her cheeks and her nails flexed against the tumbler. *It's a bit like a séance. Like being with her again for those ninety minutes.*

Oh, that's very kind. But it was the wrong thing. The actress excused herself, and Edna was alone. Her, and the club soda, and "Stormy Weather."

Then later, the movie swept through the nation's theaters. There were man-on-the-street interviews, people waiting in line to see it a fourth time, a fifth. *I love the monster*, one girl said. *He's so gross.* Marquees advertised: THE MOST FRIGHTENING FILM OF THE YEAR! Or SUBURBIA'S MONSTERS ARE ALREADY HERE! She could not open a newspaper without seeing a full-page ad. Her face reflected on the edge of a knife.

And then Wren was born. Each year's birthday party bigger than the last.

★ ★ ★

EDNA HASN'T SEEN the movie in a decade—so why tonight? Why not tomorrow, or two days ago, or on Halloween, when the local theater always screens it?

She faces the door as she watches. It's locked, a chair propped under the knob. The fear that it will swing open at any moment.

The tiniest weakness could bring down the house. If her parents had kept a better eye on them. If they hadn't been left so much to their own devices. (*How could you not have known?*) In that world, her father never would have gotten sick. It wouldn't matter so much that Roger wasn't—or, no, Roger would be here too. The center would hold, year after year.

She couldn't bear going to Starkweather yesterday. She would have tried to kill him; maybe they would have let her. (*Not a jury in the world . . .*) What is she going to do about Calla? It's been nice having her here. Another voice to share the world with. To tell them gossip and pick up milk. A third player for cribbage. But these aren't the things that make you a family. There has to be care. Trust.

Edna tries to remember which parts of the film are true and which are false. She could pick up Roger's book, measure the film against its story. Here is the record of all things that are. Here is the definite word. Oh, Roger—the scratch of his stubble, the severity of his tape recorder. She would have told him anything that made a good story. Never thinking (she was seventeen, for God's sake) she might forget.

There are days she feels that there weren't any murders. They were a theater family. It could be a performance that got out of hand. A story—a myth—told so often that it took on the ring of truth.

Or the house is evil. Or her blood is evil. Or she died and this is Hell.

Movie-Bea puts makeup on Movie-Edna. Paints her eyes, a red line on her mouth. The actress leans in so close they almost kiss.

At the premiere, Roger insisted on taking a picture of her and the Movie-Edna together. *Two sparkling diamonds*, he said. The picture came out badly, underexposed. It's wedged between the pages of Roger's book, hidden from the light for seventeen years. Indistinct, but even so. The two of them could pass for twins.

EIGHT

JAMES SPINS LEFT and right in the computer chair. His range of motion limited by the narrow room. Now you'd never guess it had been the playroom. Calla sketchily painted over the last traces of childhood—a white splash over the sun like an ugly eraser mark.

"So why do you keep doing it?" Calla asks from the bed.

"What," James says, "breathing?"

"Having sex with men. If it's not fulfilling."

"I'm sorry, are you lecturing me about unfulfilling sex?"

Calla chucks the red Solo cup, hits him dead in the forehead. Ash all over his clothes.

"Ow, fuck!"

"You get what you deserve, faggot."

"That really hurt, Calla!"

James is more surprised than hurt, but he keeps rubbing his head and *ooh*ing with pain. His attempts to dust off the ash only grind it into his clothes. He's going to spend the night smelling like a sports bar.

The thing about the boys is that they don't fuck him the right way. He doesn't know what this means or how else to say it. And it's not only the sex; when he goes to their parties, when he and Heather smoke on the couch with them, and the boys approach with their easy camaraderie, there's an enormous gulf. They might as well talk football as come in his mouth. Heather thinks he needs to loosen up. *If you knew how hot you looked drenched in sweat and come*, she said, *you wouldn't worry so much.*

When he met a girl at these parties, it took long minutes of watching to understand she was trans. She was tall and beautiful and surrounded by adoring men. She cracked joke after effortless joke. (*I prefer communion wine. In a pinch you can use it for blood play.*) That glorious gravel in her voice. He found himself staring. The fluid motion of her hands. The cotton dress that clung to her curves. And later, by the drinks table, she asked James if she could bum a cigarette. *I know we're not supposed to smoke*, she said with a wink. *But it really is the best feeling in the world.* James stammered an apology, hastened back to the couch where Heather was flirting beautiful fags into James's bed.

Sick. Guilty. What *we* did the girl mean? People? Or—or—

But James isn't. James could never be. James is normal and James is sick but James is not—is not—I mean, how would you? And where could it end but the same place St. Clouds always end?

He and Heather had taken one of the boys home. James came while the guy was buried deep inside him, covering himself in sticky shame.

To Calla he says: "Apart from all the usual reasons you have unfulfilling sex—"

"Like attention."

"—it's like anything else. You don't know where your limits are until you go past them."

Wrong answer. "*BZZZZZZ.* I don't accept that."

"Well, I don't know what to—"

"You'd know where your limits are by now."

"Maybe," James says. "Maybe not."

"Tell us the truth, Jamie. Tell your big sister."

There had been a time when she had felt like a *big* sister and not merely an older one. After Millie Quinn dumped him in tenth grade, Calla brought James to a party and fed him Smirnoff Ice until he was no longer inconsolable. She patted his back while he threw up in some upperclassman's toilet. She gave him a tiny bottle of mouthwash, a square of peppermint gum.

"Look," he says, "who knows why things have power over us? Think about—oh, I don't know, Calla. Think about Paper Bag Plastic Bag. Why did we keep doing what Edna told us? Why did we give her the power to torture Blue Bear and Pauline? It isn't like she was ripping them apart."

"She could have. She was a terror."

"She wasn't that bad."

"Yes, she was. You're too young to remember, but Roland killing all her friends is the best thing that ever happened to her."

"Every teenager is a sociopath."

"The point is," Calla says, "she was bigger than us. She wanted us in a place of subjugation and so we climbed into it. That's what you do when you're a kid. That's how you learn to be a person."

"I guess it's the same, then. Whatever this is, it's bigger than I am." James wishes Calla *would* come visit. They can't keep having these conversations on the worst night of the year. "This one time in high school, I went to Mr. Thibodeaux's room for help with physics. And as he was talking about angular momentum or whatever, I couldn't get this image out of my head—of going down on my knees and sucking him off."

"Oh, *gross*!"

"Always trust you to be sympathetic."

"Jamie, you *didn't*."

"Obviously I didn't, good fucking God. I don't know where it came from. It's not like he was hot."

"Unless you're into golfers."

"I pushed it away. It's like having the thought that you could jump off a balcony. Weird, and unsettling, but meaningless."

"I don't know," Calla says. "Maybe you really want to jump."

If it were fifty years ago, he could probably find a psychoanalyst in the Yellow Pages. Every day he'd lie on a leather couch and share his history until the man—it would be a man, with a beard—explained that it was all his mother. It was all the death drive. It was a need to blow up his entire existence. To become the thing—the monster—that held power over him for his entire life. But now everyone knows that psychoanalysis is fake. And he's stuck with his very real, unstoppable thoughts.

Calla says, "Do you think Mom and Dad were any good at being parents?"

"What?" James thinks he might have misheard her. "Of course they were." Calla doesn't say anything, only watches the half-burnt birthday candle flicker toward its end. "What do you mean?"

"I mean, do you ever talk to other people about their childhoods? Do you ever remember?"

"Is this some kind of Satanic Panic fake memory—"

"Not like that. Never mind." Calla wishes she hadn't asked—not without more to go on. There's this image of James crying, of Calla bandaging his skinned knee. She might have been five years old. The bandage wouldn't stay put, so she used two or three others to tack it in place. A dream, a memory, or someone else's story?

The questions return each time she's alone in this cursed house: Why couldn't their mom keep on living? Why didn't she give her kids a chance to say goodbye? Why would they have so much free rein except for lack of love?

Heather knocks, enters without waiting.

"There you are!" she says.

"Here I am!" James kisses her. "Have you been looking for me long?"

"Not that long. Hello, Calla."

"Hello, Heather!" she mimics.

"Calla's been telling me—" His sister shakes her head, mimes slitting her throat. "Aw, lay off it, Calla."

"It's always something with you guys," Heather says.

"She's got a *girlfriend*," James stage-whispers.

"What, in her video game?"

"No." Still stage-whispering. "In *real life*."

"Okay out, out. Get out." Calla shoos them to the door. "Wonderful as always to see you both. Same time next year? Go on, get."

ACROSS THE HALL, James's room is the same. The TV is off.

"Everything okay?" he asks.

"It's fine."

"But?"

"It's this fucking house," Heather says. "It gives me the creeps."

"'Cause of the doors?"

None of the St. Clouds talk about that June 1 morning. They told themselves it was the wind, or the house settling, or a hyperlocal earthquake. What it definitely wasn't, that was worth discussing. James will be bracing himself, come sunrise, for the house to open itself again.

"It's too big," she says. "Too quiet."

He closes the distance, gently bites her clavicle. "You think we should make some noise?" Her hands find his waist, and despite it all, she smiles.

But she says, "Do we have to come back here every year?"

"Oh, Heather."

"I want to be there for you," Heather says. "And you know I love Wren. And Edna—well, she's dealing with a lot. But there's too much here. There's something that doesn't stop."

"What are you talking about?"

"I don't know. I was in the bathroom washing up and I had the weirdest feeling."

"Cold patches of air. An electrostatic tingle. Et cetera."

"Jeez, will you listen?" James sits, hands folded on his lap. "I felt like I was being watched."

"Watched?"

"Like there was a pair of eyes behind the mirror—a little above eye level. I could tell you exactly where." She indicates, her hand roughly where any pair of St. Cloud eyes sits. "And when I went to check the basement—"

James says, "Edna never should have asked you."

"I heard breathing."

"Breathing?"

"It was this very slow inhale and exhale. Iiiiiin and ouuuuut." Maybe it wasn't breathing, but there had been something. Some soughing like the summer wind that precedes rain. The house can make any sound, any fact or feeling, sinister. It pollutes every mind that touches it.

"Heather, you have to tell Edna."

"It wasn't anything, okay? Any more than the mirror was."

"You can't be sure—"

"It's empty down there," Heather says. "I checked. Checked for all of you—your designated martyr."

"You don't get it."

"Actually, I completely get it. You act like because I didn't grow up in this gothic mess I couldn't possibly have a handle on what you're dealing with. But I know you. I get it. It's a poison. This house, this family, these stories. The ritual renewal year after year. Wearing your brother's murders on your body like some goddamn Mark of Cain."

James bites the inside of his cheek. "Take that back."

"What, am I wrong?"

"I'm not anything like him."

"I didn't say you were."

What couldn't she understand? James could change his name, flee the house, and the blood that made Roland St. Cloud would still flood his veins. The family nightmares would infect his waking life.

James says, "If you can't stand being here with me and the St. Cloud freak show, maybe you should leave."

"What?"

"Take the car. Go home."

"I'm not going to fucking leave you here."

"I mean, it's obviously *too much* for you if you're fucking *hallucinating*."

"You have to leave with me," Heather says. She won't tolerate Jamie's self-loathing, the trap of history. "You'll leave with me, and we'll go home, and we'll keep on living our lives far, far from this place. Even if we spend the rest of our lives drowning in rent, I will thank God every day this house isn't ours."

"And then what?"

"What do you mean, Jamie? We have each other, our friends. The past year has been the happiest of my life. Hasn't it for you?" James, half crying, slumps against her on the bed. She puts an arm around him. Smells the ash on him and wishes—the thousandth time tonight—for a cigarette. "Are these happy tears or sad?" He is crying almost too hard to answer.

"Don't you want to get married?" he asks between breaths. "That's what people do when they love each other, you know."

"Oh, Jamie." He sobs harder, but she can't stop now. "We get married and then what? Every night we're on the couch eating a meat and two vegetables, watching stupid prime-time sitcoms. Sometimes we have sex, but less and less. And when we do, you don't look at me. Don't make a sound. You aren't there at all. And life goes on like that, day by day, and then—what? We have kids? We keep going and this rot grows between us until one of us stabs the other in the chest?"

"Jesus Christ, Heather."

"Fuck, sorry, I didn't mean it like that. I meant—" What? That she can't give up her chair in the corner. The boys turning him inside out. Jamie—so tiny and pathetic beneath them. In the half-light, she imagines their cocks pressing against his stomach from the inside. An abject delight unlike any other. "You're nothing like them, Jamie. Any of them. You're sweet and gentle and won't kill a cockroach."

"Much to your dismay," James croaks.

"And I'll love you forever. I really will. I'll prove it to you every day and you'll prove it back. Not with rings. Not with a fucking justice of the peace, whatever that is. But with the life we make together, far from here."

Sure, James thinks. We'll make a life. You, me, and the boys. A life too crowded by half.

"We'll drive home tomorrow," Heather says, "and scrape together a dinner of grilled cheese and stale strawberry Danishes. We'll watch whatever you have from work."

"*A Matter of Life and Death*."

"Perfect. War and love and Heaven. And then we'll have a whole year to figure out what comes next, okay?"

It's a morning-mist kind of truth, dissipating under the sun's glare.

"I *have* to—" he says.

"Maybe you do, okay? Maybe you do. But we have three hundred and sixty-four days of hypothesis testing before we decide. Three hundred and sixty-four days of waking in our little golden bed. Three hundred and sixty-four days of walking by the river. An entire summer of camping in the Catskills, and fireworks in July. An autumn of crunchy leaves. A winter of cocoa and snowball fights and mitten hands. The cherry trees in spring. We have a lifetime between now and then. Okay, Jamie? Tell me it's okay."

NINE

BEFORE THE MURDERS begin, Edna ejects the disc. Slips it back into her computer. Starts over. The flickering flame behind the title, the swell of icy synths.

Calla is back in *The Neighborhood*. The Spitehouse has fallen into disrepair: cracked windows, weeds between the floorboards. She doesn't have the heart to burn the thing down. She doesn't go to the basement anymore. She's been collecting stories about other phenomena, trying to make sense of the murders: a waterfall of frogs, a photograph of a player's real dead mother, an elevator into a kind of digital Hell—fire and demons and all. That person said all the dead avatars were down there. All the people who have been murdered—and all the people who will be.

James and Heather make quiet love. Heather whispers in his ear about the men he's fucked, narrating their passion back to him. She fucks them through him, James thinks, these beautiful men who would not touch her.

Wren is in the basement—the real one. It's emptier now. Boxes of Roger's (his papers, his books, his childhood swimming trophies) were moved to storage. It's easier to see the corners. To find a cloth head with button eyes. A tiny wooden shoe. They find their way to her and she destroys them under her heel, or she tosses them into the creek. Anything to keep them from her mother's eye.

"No," she says into her flip phone, "we cooked the pizza from scratch. Mom didn't want anyone coming to the house and didn't want any of us leaving. She had the burglar alarm armed by, like, noon."

With her free hand, she guides her golem around *The Neighborhood*.

"She doesn't want me driving. I told her walking everywhere isn't any safer but—"

A pause as she listens.

"Well, if you were here, Dad, then maybe *you* could—"

Wren's golem heaves across the world. Street to street, life to life. The houses have been stripped of their logic. There are staircases at angles no one can climb. Shards of glass overhead in cheap imitation of the stars. Wren wonders how she'd feel if her avatar got killed. What she would learn. Does her bucket golem even have blood?

You must embrace the ineffable, types some digital doomsday prophet, body like a pile of clothes. *You must make a body that is unlivable, impossible, that cannot be killed. You must let the doors stay closed, for you do not want to know what they hold back. You must live on dust and dew until you see God in every pixel and then you must step into the light. The impossible body cannot be killed. This is the only soul any of us have left. The lit screen is a mirror too.*

None of this matters to Wren. If only Mieke were online. There's no thrill in examining the vault without her.

"You've spent a year apologizing," she tells her dad. At least he isn't drunk. Or, not very. "She thinks you're coming back. I won't lie, I thought you might too. This night is yours as much as it's ours."

A pause.

"I doubt it. Mom is going to be ninety and doing the ritual in her nursing home."

The murders have made people magnanimous. There's no fee now to use the mines. On a whim someone might give you a hundred thousand gold, or deed you their house. This is what the end of the world is like, Wren thinks. First comes the loving generosity. And then people will recognize there's nothing stopping them from killing.

"I'm playing *The Neighborhood*."

Pause.

"What's that mean?"

Pause.

"Yeah, Dad, I've probably read the same studies on microcommunities you have. Anyway, yes, unlike Aunt Calla I have some friends *in there*."

I have one friend, Wren thinks. I have friend.

She scrolls back through her messages with Mieke to find her phone number. As if she didn't have it memorized.

What if Wren left? Would she be just another person? Would there be eggs and toast in the morning and hangovers and dancing in the snow? She never had much interest in a life like Calla's, or James's. Never spent much time thinking about sex and marriage outside of novel plots. Maybe life didn't have to be those things. Maybe it could be—whatever this was.

"People are freaked out right now because of these murders. It's the sort of thing you could write about." She can see it now. *Fever Fever Fever: Life and Death in the Digital World* by Roger Merrilow. He wouldn't understand it, though. You had to have watched the shift happen. Fear of death leaking from one world into the other. "It's not only the real deaths that scare people," she says. "You spend hours crafting this digital self. And to have that second self permanently destroyed. It's still dying. It still bears mourning."

Pause.

"Well, it's not mourning to *you*. But for these people it is. An entire world is being remade."

Pause.

"Sure, in some ways. Foreclosure of the future. Isn't that why you left?"

Pause.

"Don't 'It's complicated' me, Dad."

Pause.

"You don't get to pawn off Mom's neuroses onto—"

Pause.

"Okay, when can I come visit?"

Pause.

"Right. Hang on a second."

Wren lowers the phone. Straining to hear—anything. There's an enormous silence in the house. Edna's movie muted. James and Heather's fucking done. Calla's eyes are too sore to go on staring at virtual funeral processions. But on the edges of the house, a girl hardly older than Wren climbs the trellis. A bottle of red wine under her arm, a gun in the waistband of her boxers.

Wren says, "I wanted to ask you something, Dad."

A year of research, a mess of contrary forum posts: Roger Merrilow, twenty-seven, and Edna St. Cloud, seventeen, pictured at the kitchen table. People say it's the greatest love story. Writing any book is an act of love. People say writing about anyone is an act of violence. Roland St. Cloud is an icon (*Slayyyy!*) or a traitor to trans people everywhere or not even really trans. People say the movie is the thing that really hurt. The book is the thing that really hurt. People say the murders themselves are the most harmful thing, all the adaptations are Roland's fault. We shouldn't call her Roland, people say. If we don't call him Roland people will think he's *actually* trans. The doll thing is creepy. The doll thing is iconic. Someone is making a dollhouse based on 507 Hackberry Road. Someone else thinks that's gross.

And the images of burned bodies. Tongues of flame leap from senseless instruments. Heat-shattered windows spit glass over city streets. People—only people—dying so that Wren could live in this enormous house.

How much horror can they be credited with?

All Wren asks is, "What happened to Roland's diary?"

Pause. Slurred equivocations.

"It was never entered as evidence in the trial, though. I've seen the transcripts."

Pause.

"They're in your office. You left quite a lot of stuff here, actually."

Pause.

"I guess I can ask her." Knowing she won't.

Her dad talks on. Wren rehearses Mieke's number. That 609 area code waiting for her. It would be so easy to call.

"Oh yeah," Wren says, "in the far, far future, on a day like today. Blah blah blah."

Pause.

"Love you, too, Dad."

TEN

SARAH HOLDS OUT the bottle to Calla, one of the four sommeliers of the apocalypse.

"I couldn't find champagne, but this looks pretty good?" she says.

"Jesus Christ, where did you get Château Pétrus this time of night?"

Sarah kisses her. "Don't worry about it, babes. Enjoy it."

"Seriously, Sarah, you aren't twenty-o—"

"I got it from my parents' place, okay?"

"Your parents?"

"I said don't worry about it. Help me open this." Sarah hands her a corkscrew. Even the cork is expensive—thick, resistant. You can feel that it spent years growing. But Calla is overzealous, or unpracticed, and the cork breaks. There is no choice but to ram the remaining half into the three-thousand-dollar bottle of wine.

Sarah doesn't notice, or care. "Cheers, babes. To our illustrious future." She pours a small stream into her lover's mouth. Swigs some herself. "God, this doesn't taste any better than Barefoot."

"Where is your folks' place?" Calla asks.

"Why does it matter?"

"You haven't mentioned it. I mean, I assumed . . ." Assumed they were estranged. That they'd kicked her out for being gay. That she had come to Calla's warm arms seeking comfort in a premature adulthood. There must be other gay people in this city, but Calla never met them. In high school and after, even the most flamboyant theater kids insisted they were straight. They fingered their girlfriends on prom night like everyone else. They were probably married now.

"The other side of the park," Sarah says.

"You don't live with them, do you?"

"I don't even speak to them." Sarah takes another swig. "How'd everything go with your brother?"

"Normal. Well, normal for Jamie."

"Does he know he looks like a fucking faggot with his hair like that?"

Calla laughs. "He'd probably like that."

"He won't tell your sister?"

"I trust him." James knew a secret's power was in its keeping.

"Cool, cool, cool." Sarah looks around the room. She's never seen the rest of the house. It could be a mirage, a hoax, a theater set. Every room plastered over like Roland's. A face without eyes or mouth or ears—no way for the world to enter.

"It's weird," Sarah says.

"What?"

"We told so many ghost stories about this place at middle school slumber parties. It's like a storybook castle. Like something we made real by talking about it." Another swig, and she pulls Calla's face to hers. Spits some wine into her mouth. The faintest hint of cherry ChapStick. Calla feels herself weaken. "It feels like we're playing a game, you know? One of those adolescent hide-and-seek games that are really excuses to be together in the dark, make out, let your hands wander across the waistband of some cute girl."

"You're still an adolescent," Calla says.

"Don't say that. You're so much better than that." Sarah looks through the ceiling like a rainmaker in a desert town. "Where should we start it?"

"Start what?" Sarah does not look her way. "Sarah, we can't burn this house down." But wouldn't it be better? They'd all be free—with no place to come back to and nothing else to lose.

"You're such a fucking bitch," Sarah says.

"Look, come—"

Sarah kicks her legs out from under her. Calla falls onto the bed and Sarah is upon her, pinning her hands to the mattress with her knees. She pours wine over Calla's face. Not quite waterboarding her; both understand that she could.

"Don't scream," Sarah says.

"Fucking get off—"

Sarah shushes her. One hand holds the bottle of Château Pétrus; the other snakes across Calla's belly, past the elastic of her underwear. It lingers at the edge of her cunt.

"I don't know," Sarah says, "why you sometimes think you're in charge here." One finger enters, then a second. Calla's moan stifled by another splash of wine. "Do you love me?"

"Stupid question," grunts Calla.

"*Do you?*"

"You know that I do."

"How do I know?"

"Get off me and we can—"

More wine. Fifty dollars of stains on the sheets.

"How do I know, little Callalily? Little flower all alone in the field. How will you prove you love me? How will you keep me from leaving?"

Sarah's fingers—long, thin, pale—worm deeper inside her.

"Please," Calla says.

"Please, what?"

"Please don't stop."

"I never have to, lover. We can have a thousand and one days and nights drinking stupid-expensive wine. I'll make you come until you think God's name is mine." Just as Calla begins to feel the white heat of orgasm's approach, Sarah withdraws. Calla whimpers. "Or," Sarah says, "we can stop. I can get what I need from anyone, Cal. I can go back to drinking Olde English in the tour van and fucking my bandmates and you can go back to—what exactly is it you were doing before?"

"Dying."

"There you go. Rotting away in a house that should be yours. This life that *you* would know how to use. Love you'd know how to keep."

"Sarah, please, come back—"

Her fingers again. Pleasure like dipping your entire body in water.

"Whose are you?" Sarah says.

"I'm yours."

"Say you will."

"I will."

"Good girl."

The wine again—slower this time. It falls into Calla's mouth and tastes like the sun. The bottle goes on the nightstand. Sarah's entire hand is inside her now, filling her up. The world is splitting. The seams of the night are so loose that a thousand blessings and terrors might filter through. A sob rises through Calla. Her body, her body, and—

"Calla?" Edna's voice from down the hall.

Sarah has the presence of mind to pull her hand out before Calla kicks—literally kicks—Sarah off her and ushers her under the bed. Calla tugs her underwear up, wipes the sweat and wine from her face.

Edna knocks. "Everything okay, Calla?"

"Yeah, fine!"

Just before Edna enters, Calla grabs the bottle.

"I thought I heard a—" Here is her baby sister, flush-faced and reeking with the ferment of sex and alcohol. "Oh!"

"I said everything is fine!"

"Your bed is a mess." Leave it to Calla to ruin the furniture. As if Edna needed more proof that her sister doesn't belong here. Not to mention: "Why the *fuck* is your window open?"

"It was stuffy," Calla says. She straightens the sheets over the wine stains. There's a phantom-limb-feeling inside her where Sarah's hand was. Every iron-filling part of her lined up to the magnetic girl beneath her bed. "Leave it to you to inherit a house without air-con—"

Edna slams the window shut.

"You know the rules."

"Yeah, yeah, yeah. Don't act like you're Mom."

"Then don't act like a child!"

Edna locks the window, runs a thumbnail over the security system wire. Had she renewed with the alarm company? Was there a short? Murderers, ghouls, monsters of all stripes could have paraded through the door. They could be in the house right now. Hiding in the basement. Waiting with their sharp knives. Waiting—

"We're going to have to check everything again," Edna says. Teeth locked on the barest sliver of tongue. She will bite it off if she has to, to keep from screaming.

"Eddie, don't you think that's an overreaction?"

Everything probably seems like an overreaction when you care so little, Edna thinks. Is Calla still capable of love? Her sister was once bright and beautiful, with bright and beautiful friends. They went on exchanging Christmas presents until Calla was twenty.

And now look at her: drunk and masturbating and God knows what else. Well, no more. A chain is only so strong, et cetera.

"Maybe this is a good time," Edna says.

"Yeah?"

Deep breath. "I know you didn't help search the house."

"Of course I did."

"The lights were still on. Just like I left them. In every room you said you checked."

"I forgot—"

"You can hear everything from downstairs, Calla. I know what your footsteps sound like."

"But—"

"Look, I liked having you back. You're good at picking movies for stormy nights and cracking jokes with Wren when we're all feeling down. It's been nice, and now I think it's time to move on."

Again the indignity, the pain, of seven years ago. Calla had sat in an oak-paneled law office and learned their parents left her and James with nothing.

"You're kicking me out?" Calla says.

"You can find another place in town. You can go back to New York."

"Out of my own house?"

"Not yours, not anymore. Not if you won't help protect it." A silence. "I love you, Calla, but you can't toy with me."

"You're such an asshole."

"How's that?"

"You were always an asshole," Calla says, "to me and Jamie. Pretending to suffocate our dolls. Burying my books in the backyard."

"I never—"

"You abandoned me at the mall," she spits, "do you remember that? You took me there to get some new earrings, said, *Be right back*, and you fucking drove home. I had to wait until a woman at the Sunglass Hut offered me a ride home. She could have been a pedo or a murderer or something worse."

"What do you want me to say? I'm sorry? Sure, I'm sorry. I was, what, sixteen?"

"I was seven, Eddie!"

"You fuck up," Edna says. "Mistakes get made; people get hurt. That doesn't mean I have to keep you in my house."

"Keep me. Like a tamed squirrel."

Edna wishes it could be different. Your friends and husband can always leave you. But your family, your blood, the curse on your name—these things are irrevocable. The story of the brother you share lights up a thousand screens across the nation, and only to you few—bound by the accidents of parentage—is it less than a story. Something as essential as the songs you grew up hearing, those black-tie opening nights. It's the ritual that makes it mean anything.

"Things were good between us, weren't they?" Edna says. "At least for a little while?"

"When was that?"

"Sometime between when you were in high school and—and when Mom and Dad died."

"We were idiots then," Calla says. "We're idiots still."

"Sure."

"It's not enough to build a life on. Not now."

"Okay." And it will be okay, Edna thinks. It'll pass. "Anyway, there isn't any rush."

"You're really kicking me out."

"It's not like you have so much stuff. I'll give you two months. I'll leave some apartment listings in the kitchen."

"I'll leave tonight."

"No, you won't."

A silence.

"I won't come back," Calla says.

"Yeah, you will. You'll need money, or a place to crash, or someone to reminisce with."

"I'll have Jamie."

"Sure. Jamie."

Calla could throw the bottle through the window. Could scream out the glass into the fresh wound of night. Could tug Sarah from under her bed and give Edna such a heart attack that—what? What would come next? She sucks down the rest of the wine.

"Well," Edna says, "I'll leave you to it. Whatever *it* is." A silence. "Don't open the window again."

Edna closes the door as she goes. And now that it's safe, now that Sarah is her only witness, Calla pitches the bottle at the door. There is a sound like a gun going off, and nothing breaks.

"Mother*fucker*," Calla spits. "Come on out."

Sarah shimmies out from the dark and the dust. Sneezes once, twice.

"So that's her in the flesh," she says. "The Ghost of Hackberry Road."

"Come on."

Calla shuts down her computer, piles up her books: Sophocles, Barthes, Sontag. There's a faded backpack in the closet that she loads everything into. Edna is right: it does not take long to pack all she owns. It takes about ninety seconds.

"You ready?" Calla asks.

"For what?"

"You heard her. We're leaving."

"And going where?"

"Your place, obviously."

A beat.

"Yeahhhh," Sarah says. "That might be difficult."

"Oh God, you do live with your parents."

"I don't normally!" Sarah is Bambi-eyed and unlined by trouble. "Clio forgot to renew our lease, and we were getting evicted. All of us live there. There's like, tons of space." Calla waits. "Whiiiich is why it totally won't be a big deal if you come stay! Okay, great."

"Great. Let's go."

"Slow down, babes. What about this house?"

"Fuck it." Calla does not want these walls to hold her ever again.

"What about our plan?" Sarah says.

"We can burn it down in a week. A month." At least I have her, Calla thinks. At least I have Sarah, so she'd better not fuck anything up.

"Let's not be hasty, okay? Your sister is treating you like dogshit. Like a newspaper wrapped around yesterday's fish. You really going to let her get away with that?"

Sarah is the only good thing that's ever happened to her.

"What's she most afraid of?" Sarah asks.

"Her brother. Intruders. The specter of death."

Sarah grins. "Well then. Let's give her the scare of her fucking life."

And for the first time, Calla can see it: the wild lick of flames. This place makes them crazy. It made their brother sick, and their father, and now Edna. It is like a song you can never quite get out of your head. It is a black spot in the middle of a brain scan. A beacon's perfect inverse—swallowing the light you would have used to call for help. They will make more light. They will leave this place unhistoried.

Calla feels the hundreds of dollars of wine, heavy in her stomach. The faint throb inside her where Sarah's fist fits perfectly. The sun will never rise; the fever will never break on its own.

"Okay," Calla says.

They leave together through the window.

ELEVEN

THE KNIFE EDNA carries isn't the same one from twenty years ago. It's about the same size—a long broken mirror of a blade that reflects the night. But it's lighter; the handle is plastic instead of wood. The blade is dull; she's neglectful of such things.

She tests the locks, rattles the windows in their casements. The spare guest room—empty. The living room—empty. Her parents' old office, the piano room—well, she rushes out of there. It's too crowded with stuff for anyone to hide.

For want of a smaller house. For want of unstoppable force and immovable object.

The plaster around her brother's door is cracking. One ear pressed to the wall; there's nothing but the sound of her own blood. Her shoulder twinges as her grip on the knife tightens. She rubs again at her scar; come morning there will be a hot bath, and daylight, and release.

For want of a life unmarked by guilt and tragedy. For want of a nonpsycho brother. Nobody ever used to joke, *So which of you is the evil twin?* There was never any question.

She doesn't know what became of that old knife. It was taken as evidence (the trial quickly over, the insanity plea a cinch; they'd used Roger's recordings instead of forcing Edna to testify), but what about after the trial? Was it buried in some basement box? Or was there some special dumping ground for murder weapons—all history's stained blades piled in a pool-size pit.

Things disappear—a knife, a room, the life you had. There was a serial-killer museum in New Orleans that wanted to buy the dress; Edna hadn't been able to find that either.

For want of a sister who fucking cared. For want of a husband who had not abandoned her. For want of friendships to replace those she'd lost. Even the Grampus, while he lived, gave Edna a sense of the world's moreness.

The downstairs bathroom—empty; you'd never guess Polly's blood once stained that tub. The cupboard under the stairs—empty. The kitchen's only life is the flickering candle. That calms her. There's the hallway and the door to the basement. Heather was just down there; surely Edna doesn't need to check it again.

She is three steps from the place she stabbed her brother, knife again ready to draw blood. That baffling, old feeling from the top of the basement steps returns to her—that she and Roland switched places. Perhaps he also felt scared, wandering through the dark. But what would a person like that be afraid of? What keeps monsters awake at night?

Roger asked her once why she was so afraid of intruders. Why brighten the darkness? Why board up the windows? The night of May 31, 1992, only proved that the threat comes from within. He didn't understand that expelling a poison doesn't make you immune to it. You have to go on protecting what you have.

And look at her now! Checking the whole house herself. Protecting every person she loves. Air and darkness part before her like a sea before a prophet. She doesn't need Roger, or James, or any of them—and because she doesn't, she can choose to keep them. When the morning comes, she'll apologize to Calla. Invite her to put the candle outside. That's always Edna's favorite part: fire's light meeting the day. The freedom morning brings.

She'll invite her sister to stay. There'll be stipulations—Calla won't be trusted to search the house again—but it's better to have everyone home. In this house their grandfather built, its walls stronger every year.

Edna will remind Calla of the good. The time she'd gotten the stomach flu, and Edna had tucked her into bed, made tomato soup, sang her Beatles songs until she fell asleep. Edna had driven her to college. Edna had gotten Calla's first play produced. All that counted for something, didn't it?

She hasn't moved from the basement door. She doesn't need to check down there. If something bad happened, it would come from the attic, the chimney, the flower beds outside. Anywhere but the basement.

Edna holds her breath. Tightens her grip on the knife. Opens the door.

There are the stairs. The darkness.

TWELVE

HEATHER AND JAMES lie in bed, spent and naked. Springsteen's *Nebraska* plays on an old turntable. James is very still beside her.

How do you reconcile what you want from the world and what it wants from you? How do you measure your wanting, James wonders, and ask for the things that feel good, and get them, and keep getting them?

"What's wrong?" Heather asks.

"What? Nothing."

"You're so bad at lying."

"I'm not lying, I just—" He can solve this. "I don't think things can keep going this way." A beat. "I love you so much, Heather, but—but we need to think about where we're headed. Where we end."

"Hold on." She stands, James's childhood quilt around her bare shoulders. She lifts the tonearm and the music stops and—

"Please don't turn it off."

—Heather drops it, probably scratching the record. The music returns in the middle of a different song.

"Spit it out, Jamie."

"I don't want to break up."

"That's great. I don't want to either. Now tell me what you do want."

She can't return to the bed until this ends. They have to decide what comes next.

"We've been going in circles," James says. "Maybe that's what being alive is. Every day you'll meet me at the video store with almond croissants and PB and J macarons. I'll bring home something by Fassbender or Hitchcock, and we'll watch it cuddling on the couch."

He is asking without asking, Heather thinks. A reprise of his marriage proposal. What a miserable idea, that they should give up the wonders of the past year. "That isn't all life is," she says.

"And every now and then, I'll put on a skirt and you'll fuck me in the ass." James is breathless. "But please, no more bars and nice boys with pretty eyes. No more bringing them home. I can't keep lying there while they're pounding away, wondering, *What if this is all Heather wants? What if she never lets me touch her again?*"

"I'll always—"

"There isn't any always, H. Nothing goes on forever. It's like taking a balloon up very, very high. Eventually the air stops, and it's all sky. And you can't breathe the sky, Heather." He's crying now and desperately hopes Heather won't move to comfort him. "I mean, am I going to have to go on like this forever so that everyone else can get their fucking rocks off?"

"That's enough. That's enough, James." All he has to cover himself with is a sheet; he wears it to his chest. "Why are you acting like this?"

"Like a freak. A monster."

"No, like a jerk." Heather sees herself veer off course, into her own grievances, and she does not stop. "Like everyone else in this house—too busy with their problems to remember that there is an outside. That there's actually a whole goddamn world. Even your niece—who is, by some enormous stroke of luck, wonderful—doesn't seem to know that."

"She had a very easy childhood," he says.

"You had an easy childhood! Look at this fucking place!"

"You don't know what it's like to grow up in the shadow of—"

"I do, though! I do, Jamie, because I listen to what you tell me. *All us St. Clouds are monsters waiting to be born*, blah blah blah. You guys do your goddamn ritual every year and somehow *never* realize that it traps you. It pins you to the miserable fucking story you've been telling your entire life."

"And what would you have us do instead, huh? Forget?"

"Get better therapy," she says, "or join a support group or change your name and move far away and don't—look—back."

"You are breaking up with me," James says.

"Maybe I am. I think that's up to you, Jamie. I think you have to pick what happens next."

On the stereo, Springsteen sings about how everything that dies someday comes back. Let them make it home, Heather thinks. Let them return to the boys, the chair, the sweat. One domino and then the next.

"Fine," he says.

"Fine?"

"Let's leave now. Let's not spend another dawn here."

"James."

"It's—it's whatever." He tries to smile. Heather is still standing, and he is still on the bed. "They're my family, Heather."

"They can come to us."

"They won't."

"Life is long, Jamie. People do all kinds of things."

THIRTEEN

WREN DOESN'T THINK as she punches in the ten numbers. This must be how it feels to kill or kiss or die. A thing is impossible and in the next breath it's done.

"Mieke! Hi!" Wren's heart won't shut up. The pulse of blood at her core, the rush in her ears. On the computer screen, the bucket golem stands in this same basement. The game's breathing sounds match her own.

Mieke laughs; for a moment, Wren is terrified. "Right on the first try," Mieke says. "You wouldn't believe how many people think my name is *Mike*."

Mieke's honeyed voice lands somewhere between tenor and alto. Of course, Wren thinks. Of course she's trans.

"What are you up to?" Wren asks.

"I was hanging out with some friends on the quad," Mieke says. "The year's over but we're sticking around for summer school. We were going to have a firefly-catching contest but *someone*"—her voice directed away from the phone, laughing—"forgot to bring jars." Protests from afar.

"I'm sure the fireflies enjoy having an ally on the inside." Wren bites her cheek. Afraid she'll say the wrong thing and not wanting Mieke to ever stop talking. "Anyway, I don't want to distract you from your friends."

"No, it's fine, they're dead to me. Oh! And I have something to show you. One second." The lines dies. Wren mutes her computer, listens to the air around her. She gets up, clears the boxes from the middle of the floor. No vault. Nothing.

For Mieke, it's any other night. Adirondack chairs and lightning bugs flying free. Lights blink on and off without any intimation of living or dying. Only light-dark-light-dark.

When Wren returns to her computer, Mieke's there beside her golem. A-line dress and ultramarine nails. Wren would bet anything this is exactly how she looks.

How'd you know I'd be here? Wren writes.

MiekeShaw: *Lucky guess :)*

MiekeShaw: *I wish you could come hang out! My friends would really like you!*

MiekeShaw: *You could visit this summer :)*

Wren fights to swallow. What if Mieke finds out who she is, what family she's from, and hates her for it? Could Wren live with it if people have used Roland's name as an attack against her? Could she ever come back to this house?

That'd be great, she writes. *I'll bring the firefly jars.*

MiekeShaw: *omg hahahahahaha*

MiekeShaw: *and we could go to the Central Park Zoo! they have red pandas!!*

I'd love that, Wren writes. Again, that ease like dying. *What did you want to show me?*

MiekeShaw: *OH!*

MiekeShaw: *RIGHT!*

Mieke's avatar—that average blonde girl—walks to the vault. She crouches over the door and spins the brass wheel. There is a sound like a thousand coins clicking. There is a release. The door eases open a crack.

And there it is—the breathing. Quiet at first as a distant train. Louder, and nearer, and louder still. Wren turns down the volume and still it's too loud. The speakers vibrate with its exhalation; whatever horrid thing has such a set of lungs will shake this house to pieces.

But no thing comes. It is the breathing and the breathing alone. It rises, past girl and golem, past the dingy walls of the digital house. Rises through the living room's weedy floorboards, the bedroom with its stained cot, the mouse-filled attic. It is far above and they can still hear it and still it rises, rises, until it vanishes.

MiekeShaw: *do you want to see what's behind the door?*

HOW DID YOU DO THAT! No pretense of coolness now. *YOU'RE A MAGICIAN*, Wren types. *A WITCH! ASDFASDFGDASF*

MiekeShaw: *sometimes we invest things with too much power :)*

YES PLEASE OPEN IT

MiekeShaw: *you do the honors*

MiekeShaw: *just*

What?

MiekeShaw: *sometimes this game can be cruel*

The vault door is heavy. The speakers creak as it sinks, bobs up, sinks. In the end, Mieke has to help. The heavy brass swings back and—well, Wren's already guessed.

Beneath the vault door lies nothing.

Not a hole, or a depthless black tile, or some sort of twisting mystery.

There's nothing there. There's the basement's concrete floor, and that's all.

MiekeShaw: *aw sorry friend :(this is what I meant*

But Wren doesn't send back a response. Her laughter fills the basement to its corners.

FOURTEEN

EDNA IS AT the top of the stairs, knife in hand, when she hears the laughter. Her blood runs cold. It's a cliché, a borrowed emotion, but there are no other words for the body's icy halt. Hypothermically sealed until the world turns far enough that we learn to thaw it.

She recognizes the laugh, but that doesn't soothe her. Anything might be a trick; anyone might be a monster. She enters the basement knife-first.

More laughter. The image of Bea's body, thrown left and right. The knife in her eye. Edna takes one careful step and another.

The laughter stops.

"Mom?"

Another step. The basement sprawl will be visible in two more.

"Mom, you're scaring me. Say something."

A step and a step and—there she is. There's her daughter.

"Oh my god, Wrennie, I was so frightened."

"Sorry, Mom."

Laughter dribbles out and Wren covers her mouth, embarrassed.

"What are you doing down here?" Edna asks. Doesn't she know it isn't safe? Doesn't she know what the darkness hides?

"Um. Sitting. It's cozy down here." One final laugh escapes. "That probably sounds weird."

"No, no." Look at it, after all. Some cardboard boxes. A stained concrete floor. The bathroom that was her first darkroom. She'd strung up pictures of her parents, and Bea, and winter wood self-portraits. Snow speckling her hair. She was so young then. Younger than Wren and half as smart.

Edna hugs Wren. The sitting girl and her standing mother fold awkwardly together. But it is warm. It is safe.

"Mom, why do you have a knife?"

"You know how it is."

They're both laughing now. They do not release their embrace.

"Mom? I want to start looking at colleges this summer."

"We'll talk about it, sweetie." It's too much to think about now. Even Charlottesville is so far away. She can't lose anyone else.

"Maybe NYU?"

"Some other time."

"Okay. I mean it, though. It would be good—"

"I mean it too. But not tonight, love." Anything for this conversation to end. For them to hold each other, and hold each other, and hold each other. The house could crumble above them and they'd still be safe in this concrete bunker.

"Okay," Wren says.

They go on holding.

UPSTAIRS: THERE ARE no monsters in the guest room, the piano room, under the stairs. There are the plywood barriers in the living room. There is the candle in the kitchen. There is no evil in the world; certain places are just wrong.

Sarah kicks open the front door. She and Calla have ski masks and bright-red gas cans. They splash gasoline across the hallway, the living room rug, the shelf of books and movies and the St. Cloud parents' plays. All their stories will burn.

It's good, thinks Calla. It's right. Fire built this house and fire will be its end. They may come here in dreams but never again in life—not even to visit the ruins. They will be free.

Calla tugs off her ski mask. "God, I can barely breathe."

"I love the smell, babes. Ever since I was little."

"You were probably a little firebug, weren't you?"

Sarah kisses her, bites her lip. "Be a good girl and put your mask back on."

Calla does. "Make sure to leave a path to the back door. We don't want—"

"Way ahead of you," Sarah says, and goes on pouring.

JAMES AND HEATHER pack their things.

"I figure I can drive the first four hours," Heather says, "and we can switch for the back four? That way you can sleep."

"None of us sleep tonight, Heather."

"That'll change. One day May 31 is going to be a day like any other."

"I'll take the first shift."

A silence.

"So are we ever getting married?" James asks.

"I said I'd always love you."

"You said a lot of things, H. You'll have to forgive me if I can't keep track of which ones you mean."

"Jamie—"

"What proof do I have that I won't wake up five years from now with no family and no girlfriend and nothing to my name but a closetful of skirts that don't fit my stupid straight hips? What do you think I'd do in that situation? I think I'd put a bullet in my brain."

Through grit teeth: "Sure. Let's get married. Why not." And if they do, and if it changes everything, they'll find a path forward. Heather knows the St. Clouds, for all their talk of curses, always pull through. "You know," she says, "if you want to be a girl—"

"Yeah, yeah. I can kill a couple and hope my soul takes over their bodies."

THE GROUND-FLOOR COMMOTION startles Edna and Wren from their embrace.

"It's probably Uncle James," Wren says.

Edna shushes her.

IF YOU SQUINT, the gasoline's path could make an enormous X. From the open front door, across the entryway, through the guest room, the hallway, and Wren's room. Into the living room, the dining room, the kitchen. Profane vertices in an act of rage. Every door is barred by accelerant. Calla will wonder at this later. If Sarah ever intended to survive.

On the kitchen table burns the final candle. Sarah stands on an untouched patch of linoleum. Soup pot and wooden spoon in hand. A flush in her cheeks. They could stop here. The promise of fire without fire itself. They could fuck until dawn in Sarah's parents' basement. Never again lend their shadows to this house's darkness.

"You ready for this?" Sarah asks.

And Calla nods. Freedom is coming. Their history will escape into the clouds.

The spoon beats against the pot. A clangor like Hell's bells at the end of days.

"Come on out!" Sarah shouts. "Come out all you St. Cloud cunts! It's showtime you motherfuckers. The game is on."

THE CLAMOR REACHES every room.

Heather: "What on Earth?"

James: "I know that voice."

"WREN," EDNA SAYS. "Stay put."

"But, Mom—"

"No. Listen. Hide behind those boxes and do not come out for *anything*."

"I'm not a child anymore."

"It doesn't matter," Edna says. Safety is a myth. Even in her daughter's embrace, her grip on the knife has not loosened.

The basement door is cracked open. Edna moves toward it one step at a time.

JAMES AND HEATHER reach the bottom of the stairs, and the smell is overpowering.

"Oh God, what happened?" Heather says. Thinking: an accident. Somehow a car broke down in the living room. The boundaries muddled between inside and outside, car and street, human and machine.

"Don't touch the floor," James says. Sarah goes on ringing her pot. The insistent beat of dread and danger. James and Heather crane their necks to see into the kitchen.

"Who the fuck is *that*?" Heather asks. James doesn't answer. How eager Calla looks in the candlelight.

★ ★ ★

EDNA INCHES HER way up. She does not hear the voices or the banging. All she hears is the house creaking. The basement's twenty-years-gone tumult. Her brother's inhuman howl as her knife missed his heart.

SARAH SPIES JAMES and Heather. Through the dark, they are indistinct. All she sees is the feminine forms and all she thinks is that her quarry has arrived.

"How do you like this," she calls, "you stupid cunt? You can't keep what isn't yours."

Sarah throws down her pot with a final clang. Lifts the candle from the table.

"Sarah," Calla says, "that's not—"

Candle hits gas. Yellow flame runs from kitchen to dining room. Living room, Wren's, the piano room, the guest room. All the dark corners, so carefully checked for the past's horrors, are alight again. There is no shadow that can hide from these autumn-leaf flames. The Earth goes on turning. A window in the piano room shatters. There is unbearable warmth on every face. The house is ablaze.

AND THEN IT isn't.

NO ONE WILL ever agree what happened. There is a noise that might be the front door slamming. There is a sound like the slow exhale of enormous lungs. A wind moves through the house. But the heat is gone. The light. It is as though the fire, having burned through its accelerant, found no further nourishment. Come morning, the only proofs of flame will be the broken window and a trail of char. It will be scrubbed away as blood is, with soap and cold water.

Sarah's ragged shriek tears out of her. "*NO.*" She tugs the gun from her waistband as Heather rounds the corner. Sarah doesn't care at whom she aims; she will shoot each St. Cloud through the heart and burn this house again.

The gun's flash; Heather falls, clutching her shoulder.

"Heather!" James runs to her, presses the wound. He loops his belt around her arm as Sarah lines up a second shot.

Calla inventories what might be left to her in the morning: a game, a name, a short writing career. Will Sarah still love her? Will that love be good? Calla doesn't think she'll pull the trigger twice. No one is supposed to die tonight.

THE FIRST THING Edna notices is how much the girl looks like Bea. Maybe she didn't die at all; Roland's ritual worked—not how he planned it, but it worked. Bea is here and she is going to punish Edna for letting her come to harm. She is going to tell Edna that she loves her. They will be sixteen again, listening to Nirvana on Bea's Walkman—heads side by side, each pressed to one scratchy headphone. It's a terrible way to listen to music, and neither will give it up.

But here is the smell of fire and gasoline. Here is James's girlfriend writhing on the floor, and red stains on her Kate Bush T-shirt. James crouches over her, crying. Calla, with an uncertain sickness in her eyes. Edna sees it all as if illuminated by some bright new star. She sees the gun, and she stops thinking.

FOR A YEAR after this, maybe two, no one goes anywhere.

Heather's shoulder heals; she and James haunt the house, watch stupid horror movies in his bedroom, and don't touch. There are more circling, aborted conversations.

Every time Calla looks at the front door, she's hit with the sick stink of gasoline. If she'd chosen differently, would she be in Sarah's arms now? Soft and safe in some motel bed a million miles from here? One day, everyone logs in to *The Neighborhood* to find their avatars dismembered, FEVER scribbled over their walls. Some people try to rebuild, but the game never really recovers. It is no less a death than dying; anything you give attention to is alive. In Calla's dreams, she is still in the game. An avatar that looks like Sarah is bleeding out on the basement floor. When she wakes, she starts to write again.

What Wren remembers most is those minutes spent waiting. The second gunshot's report. Not knowing. It feels like vertigo—like she might fall into an ordinary scrap of floor. After everyone is asleep, she wanders in the woods. Tree trunks like night made solid. She does not need *The Neighborhood* now that she calls Mieke most days. The sound of the other girl's voice is like the night sky—vast and comforting and pricked with light.

Journalists and true-crime writers reach out to Edna, James, Calla, even Heather. Among them is a sheepish Roger. Things aren't going well with Diana Cutter, or his new book, and does Edna want to chat about what happened?

Of course, in the aftermath of calamity, Edna will want everyone home.

Roger is the only one who speaks to Sarah's parents. The scale of the Fletchers' house rivals the St. Clouds'—a new darkness in its corners. Roger listens to Whileaway demos, transcribes snatches of lyrics: *My sex is not a costume, you can't buy my cunt online. Don't come near me with your rapist hands and we'll all! Be! Fine!* Her friends say there was always something intense about her. She knew hurt from both sides. Roger records the dates she ran away from home and the dates she came back. Her high school art teacher will talk about her suicide attempts. Feeding the story. Watching it grow.

A year. Maybe two. And then they start to leave. Wren, then Heather, Jamie, Calla. Roger. They find new loves, or maintain the old. They're comforted by warm flesh or the cool emptiness beside them in bed. They have seen the lightning strike of their family's violence; like lightning, you are more likely to be struck a second time, a third. This is a death they cannot mythologize. This is a death they must all mythologize together. It binds them as it drives them from here.

One day, Edna will stand alone in the four-candled dark. She will recall the feeling of knife in flesh, which let her leave home once before. And when she goes, the house will stand empty for years. Invaded by reckless children with cans of spray paint and porn magazines. They will tell one another stories that spiral, contradict, and transform under the spell of each new tongue. The St. Cloud name will be called through broken windows and etched into the plaster outline of a hidden door. And none of them—not Edna, not Jamie, Calla, Roger, or Wren—will be there to hear its echo.

BUT FIRST: EDNA bursts from the basement. But first: Sarah sees her and shifts her aim. Calla sees the knife in Edna's hand and recognizes: there is no good outcome here—only the least bad. She'll spend years understanding why she does it. The best she comes up with is the memory—the dream, the story—of her younger brother's scraped knee. St. Cloud blood staining a paper towel as she tries, futilely, to allay his crying. It's war that moves the world. War and capital.

Calla thrusts a hand under Sarah's and pushes. The shot buries a bullet over the kitchen door. The knife is in Sarah's chest. Edna pushes it deeper. There are no ghosts, no demons, no ghouls. There is only Edna, and her siblings, and their lovers. There is her daughter in the basement. There is her wretched brother, with his scar that matches hers—proof she is able to cut. That she can regret not taking a life. Edna drives the knife in again. There is a wet rattle in Sarah's chest and a smile on her face. Pleased that she will get a kind of immortality. She will be her own ghost story, passed in whispers at every slumber party in town. For a final time, the knife closes the distance between them. Sound returns to Edna: James's pleas, Heather's reassurances. Calla's steady, bewildered breathing. Edna feels Sarah dying. Slipping into that measureless place. And for one second, she must fight the urge to carve an X into the girl's chest. Take me from here, she thinks. Give me a new life—give me whatever. But there are no miracles or curses here. The girl is dying. The sun is coming up. A new day dawns over the same house, the same family as before.

INTERTEXTS

This would be a different work without the influence of the following:

Men, Women, and Chain Saws: Gender in the Modern Horror Film by Carol J. Clover

Corpses, Fools and Monsters: The History and Future of Transness in Cinema by Caden Mark Gardner and Willow Catelyn Maclay

Playing Real: Mimesis, Media, and Mischief by Lindsay Brandon Hunter

My Tiny Life: Crime and Passion in a Virtual World by Julian Dibbell

Savage Appetites: Four True Stories of Women, Crime, and Obsession by Rachel Monroe

The Journalist and the Murderer by Janet Malcolm

A Mother's Reckoning: Living in the Aftermath of Tragedy by Sue Klebold

Halloween (2018), dir. David Gordon Green

Still Walking (2008), dir. Hirokazu Kore-eda

Mysterious Skin (2004), dir. Gregg Araki

Yi Yi (2000), dir. Edward Yang

Twin Peaks: Fire Walk with Me (1992), dir. David Lynch

Written on the Wind (1956), dir. Douglas Sirk

Ranged Touch's *Game Studies Study Buddies*, *Just King Things*, and *Homestuck Made This World*

ACKNOWLEDGMENTS

Thanks to my agent, Danielle Bukowski, and my editor, Mo Crist—I cannot imagine a better team to bring this book into the world. Thanks to everyone else at Bloomsbury: Rosie Mahorter, Katie Vaughn, Valerie Burke, Barbara Darko, Laura Phillips, Eleanor Peters, Myunghee Kwon, Andrew Nguyen, and Jennifer Choi, as well as Logan Hill and Gleni Bartels. Thanks to Charlie Sorrenson, who reassured me it wasn't evil. Thanks to Emet North for continuing to keep me sane. Thanks to every bookstore that hosted an event for *Still Life* and thanks to every friend who let me crash on their couch. Thanks to Creekbed Carter Hogan, whose live shows gave me St. Margaret. Thanks to Asher Ford, Ever Hayward, Alice Stoehr, Erica Clashe, Natalie Marlin, and everyone else who has helped make Minneapolis home. Thanks to Ana Poole, Ginger Bloomer, and Gary Poole for always making me feel like a part of the family. Thanks to the Burke-Packert-McIntoshes, who take care of their own. Thanks to Mom and Dad for always taking us to the theater. Thanks to Chris for liking the same kind of schlock I do. Thanks to Justin Saret for always having questions. Thanks to Rae Beaudoin and Kevin Norwood for putting my name on their guest room door. Thanks to Andy Cawley and Erik Baker for more than a decade of friendship and for making me ever more David Lynch–pilled. Thanks to Simone Scott, my sister in Christ. And thanks to Gabi, for every single day.

A NOTE ON THE AUTHOR

KATHERINE PACKERT BURKE's debut novel, *Still Life*, was published by W. W. Norton in 2024. She lives in Minneapolis, Minnesota.